KNIGHTS OF THE LOST DOMAIN

Julian Atterton has a passion for early and medieval English history. He has written six adventure novels set between the sixth and the fourteenth centuries – in the ancient kingdom of Northumbria, which encompasses the part of Yorkshire where he now lives. When not writing he spends a good deal of time researching his subject. "I like my fictions to have truth," he says. His novels are stories, though, not historical tracts. "What matters most," he says, "is the magic of reading-time – the escape from our day-to-day cares provided by immersion in the fiction – which is as rich in any genre."

Although a complete story in itself, *Knights of the Lost Domain* is also the second book in a trilogy that began with *Knights of the Sacred Blade*. The author's other books are *The Last Harper*, *Fire of the Kings* (both shortlisted for the Young Observer Teenage Fiction Prize), *The Tournament of Fortune* and three stories for younger children, *The Shape-Changer*, *Robin Hood and the Miller's Son* and *Robin Hood and Little John*.

CONTENTS

I n the year 1138, King David of the Scots invaded Northumbria with fire and sword.

Cumbria was overrun, Northumberland was lost, and the holy city of Durham besieged; but when the Scots crossed the Tees they were met by an army under the banners of three saints, and it was there, at the Battle of the Standard, that they were at last defeated and thrown back.

The Scottish advance had been broken, but half Northumbria remained in their hands. When the English begged King David for peace, he was willing to grant it only if he could keep all he had won.

This was more than King Stephen could accept, and the war might have been endless had not a settlement been found to which both kings could agree. It was that David's son should rule in Cumbria and Northumberland, and in return swear an oath of loyalty to King Stephen.

On the day King David agreed to the terms, a truce was proclaimed throughout Northumbria; but it takes more than a truce to end a war.

PART ONE
The Bewitched

1. KNIGHTHOOD'S VOW

I was woken by the bells of York, though it was a moment before I recognised them.

In my dream I had rushed ahead to the journey's end and Adele, only to find that in the two weeks I had been gone she had ridden away with a knight to a distant land, no one knew where.

So it was good to wake in the loft of the hostel on the staith where the archbishop had given us lodging, and catch the smell of fresh bread wafting up from the hearth below. By the time I had dressed and clambered down the ladder, the fear of losing Adele that had spoken through my dream had given way to the excitement of knowing I would be with her by sunset.

My father was nowhere to be seen, and half his men were asleep or falling asleep, for they had been feasting all night on the long-promised city. Orm was outside, sitting on a barrel with his fur cloak to keep out the chill of the winter morning.

"Where is Jordan?" I asked him.

"Gone to Mass," said Orm. "We're to be ready when he returns."

"Have we time for a walk down the street of the

silversmiths?" I asked. "I want to find a gift for Adele."

The old Viking gave me a sidelong glance. "How long have you been buying gifts for Adele Espec?" he asked.

"Now I am a knight," I said, "I can begin. I owe her a gift for nursing me back to life after the Battle of the Standard."

Orm opened his mouth to speak, then thought better of it and stared out over the river.

"Go on," I told him. "Spit it out. Tell me she is too good for the likes of me."

"It's not that," said Orm with a shrug. "I was thinking of that lass who came to find you in Northumberland."

I looked at him reproachfully, then realised how separate our paths through the war had been, and how much there still was to tell him of mine.

"Catriona," I said. "That is her name. I do not even know where she is."

Orm read the rest in my face. "I did not mean to stab you in the heart," he said. "Let's take that walk to the silversmiths."

We had not gone far when I heard Aimeric calling my name and saw his black-sleeved arm waving at me across the street. A moment later the thin scholar was at my side.

"Thurstan wants us," he said breathlessly.

"Jordan has gone to Mass," I told him.

"It is not your father he wants," said Aimeric. "He wants you – you and me."

"Why?" I asked. "Everything was said last night. What is wrong?"

Orm laughed. "One of the kings must have gone back on his word."

"Do not even say it in jest," Aimeric begged him, and I

shared his dread. We ourselves had witnessed King David's agreement to make peace, and we had been spreading the word as we rode south. To be thrown back now into war would be unbearable.

"Do you truly not know why Thurstan wants us?" I asked.

Aimeric spread his hands. "His chaplain told me to find out if you were still in the city. That is all I know."

"On your way, then," said Orm, clapping me on the shoulder, and I hurried anxiously with Aimeric towards the archbishop's palace.

"Surely there is no one evil enough to break the treaty?" I asked, though even as I spoke I thought of the one man we knew who was.

"Do not even call it a treaty," warned Aimeric. "It is a truce, but no more. It will not be a treaty until it is signed and sealed and the law in both kingdoms."

"When will that be?" I asked.

"That," said Aimeric balefully, "is what still has to be agreed."

We made our way through the lower halls of the palace and climbed to the chamber where Thurstan's illness now forced him to spend much of his days. His chaplain was warding the door, but as soon as he saw us he knocked, lifted the latch and swung it open for us to enter.

Thurstan was sitting in a tall chair by the window with a lady's fur-trimmed riding-cloak spread over his knees. Its owner was standing beside him with her back to the thin November light, so that at first glance I could make out only a faceless figure in a crumpled linen coif and a mud-splashed grey gown. There was no one else in the room.

"Here is Simon de Falaise," Thurstan told her, "and this is Aimeric the scholar. Last night they brought me a treasure we have been seeking for three years, and if ever it is safe for the story of their quest to be told, they will be famous men. For the moment it is enough for them that their friends know their worth. Make them your friends and they will not fail you."

I bowed to the lady with all the courtesy Adele had taught me, but she gave no sign of being impressed. "This is the knight of your choice?" she asked Thurstan. "He seems very young."

Thurstan smiled. "In years but not in experience," he told her. "Simon fought like a lion in the Battle of the Standard. He has fought against King David so nobly that David himself bestowed knighthood on him, on the very day the terms of peace were agreed."

I blushed with pride, for in the three years I had served the archbishop I had come to love him. His praise was worth more to me than gold.

"Tell me, Simon," he asked, "when you took knighthood, what was your vow?"

"To be a shield to widows and orphans," I replied, "to protect holy Church, and to draw my sword only when justice demands it."

"Then may God walk with you," said Thurstan warmly, "for those are the words Odilo of Cluny of blessed memory gave for those to whom knighthood is a quest of the spirit and not a life of plunder. I know you, Simon; I know you will be true to your vow."

It was always the same with Thurstan. I knew my weaknesses, but he reached past them to my spirit, and I wanted so much to believe his words. His own courage shone all the more keenly now his body was so frail and we could see the battle he had to fight every day. I felt as if I could see the candles glowing in the aisles of his mind, their light a white magic that filled me with strength.

"It is to be a shield to an orphan I call on you now," he said. "How long is it since you rode to Cumbria?"

Cumbria – the very name made me catch my breath. "A year, my lord. It was just before the war broke."

"I must ask you to go back," said Thurstan. "This lady is Maud de Rumilly of Allerdale-above-Derwent. I want you to be her guardian. I want you to escort her home."

I glanced at the lady with a sudden understanding of her misgivings. If it was a guardian she needed, I fell a long way short of the Archangel Michael.

"Your father is bound for Elmeslac, I believe?" Thurstan asked me. "It might be best if you took Maud with you."

Maud knelt and took the archbishop's hand. "Do not make me wait," she implored him.

"You can leave as soon as I have gathered the companions for your road," he told her.

"Then keep me here with you," she begged.

Thurstan laughed with pure delight. "My child, you cannot stay in a palace full of priests. Your beauty would bewitch them. If you truly cannot face the world, the sisters of Clementhorpe would give you shelter, but it would comfort me to think of you in Elmeslac. I will summon you as soon as Bishop Aethelwold is here."

Maud bent her head and kissed the blue sapphire of Thurstan's ring, and as she rose she took the riding-cloak from his knees and fastened it around her shoulders. I knelt in turn, and as I stood up Thurstan fixed me with his gaze.

"I entrust her to you, Simon," he said, "but I forbid you to ask her what brought her to me."

"He must be told," protested Maud.

"I forbid you to tell him," Thurstan said firmly.

I was too lost for words to protest. It astonished me that he could entrust me with her life but not the story of it. Maud de Rumilly clearly agreed, and at least my confusion moved her to speak to me gently.

"Simon de Falaise," she said, "I will be grateful for your escort."

When we stepped out into the palace yard I saw that she was fair and in the bloom of youth – but she was milk-faced with weariness.

"Where are your servants and escort?" I asked her.

"I rode to York alone," she said. "I left my horse with the grooms."

Aimeric and I exchanged glances of frustration as it dawned on us what it was to be forbidden to ask more. We stood in silence until Maud's horse was led out, a fine grey palfrey, and I held her stirrup for her to mount.

Aimeric kissed me on the cheeks. "Take her to Adele," he whispered. "Adele will care for her."

"Are you ready to return to Cumbria?" I asked him.

"I will try to be," he said without conviction. "I have been back so often in my nightmares that perhaps I need to return in daylight."

For a moment I was bewitched by my own memories – for it was in Cumbria that I had learnt the depths of love and hate – but I shook them off and bid Aimeric farewell, hooked my fingers into the horse's bridle and led Maud de Rumilly out into the city.

I took her by way of the street where the kings of old had had their halls and now the merchants bustled. The gown-makers and furriers called out to her from their shops, but she did not even look tempted.

"York is a rich city," she remarked, almost as if she disapproved.

"You should have seen this street on the eve of the Battle of the Standard," I told her. "It was boarded and shuttered. Everyone had fled. The merchants did not believe we could save the city from the Scots."

"I thank God you did," said Maud, "but why did you not follow it by driving the Scots from Northumberland and Cumbria?"

"It was beyond our strength," I said, "and it will be until King Stephen comes north to lead us."

"He will not come," said Maud, and she said it bitterly, as if she were certain, and as if she felt betrayed. "I have forgotten," she said, "where are you taking me?"

"To Elmeslac, the castle of Walter Espec."

"He is your lord?" she asked.

"My father held a castle in Northumberland for him," I explained. "It was besieged from the first day of the war until the last, when its surrender was a part of King David's price for peace."

"Your father must have found that a hard price to pay," said Maud thoughtfully.

"Here he is," I told her, for we turned a corner to see Jordan riding over the bridge towards us. Orm was at his side, leading my horse by the reins, and behind them straggled a somewhat bleary cavalcade, their faces marked less by a year under siege than by the last night's revelry – but their shoulders went back and their eyes cleared when they caught sight of Maud.

"What have we here?" Jordan asked me. "Has Thurstan found you a wife?"

"He has entrusted me with this lady," I said. "Her name is Maud de Rumilly, and she is riding with us to Elmeslac."

"Then I will be honoured if you would ride at my

side," Jordan told her, and he all but snatched her from my hands and carried her off, leaving me to swing up into my own saddle and trot behind them through the jostle of the narrow streets.

"Hold out your hand," Orm told me.

I obeyed and he dropped into my palm a pouch of blue cloth sealed with a pin. It chinked in my grasp, yet it weighed almost nothing.

"What is it?" I asked.

"A gift worthy of Adele Espec," he said. "Moorish bracelets, thin as a blade of grass but each with their own pattern."

I gazed at him gratefully. "They must be beautiful," I said. "What do I owe you?"

"Nothing," he said. "You saved my brother from William FitzDuncan. I'll not forget."

"And you taught me all the swordcraft I know," I replied. "If it comes to debts – "

Orm winked and changed the subject. "Tell me what Thurstan had to say."

"He has made me Maud de Rumilly's guardian. He wants me to escort her home."

"I can think of worse tasks," said Orm. "Where does she live?"

"Allerdale-above-Derwent," I said. "Do you know it?"

"In Cumbria?" asked Orm, turning on me. "Thurstan would send you back?"

"Last time, I went against his orders," I reminded him. "Aimeric and I were alone. Thurstan did not even know where we were."

"It was a bold ride," said Orm, "which is why it might be pushing your luck to try it again so soon."

"This time, we will not be alone," I said. "We will be riding with Bishop Aethelwold."

"The protection of the Church," muttered Orm, in a voice that fell short of awe. "So who is Maud de Rumilly?" he asked. "Why does she need an escort?"

"I do not know," I confessed.

"You must know who she is."

"Only her name."

Orm looked at me incredulously. "Thurstan said nothing? He simply gave her to you?"

"He has forbidden me to ask more. You have only to look at her to see she is spent. Whatever brought her to Thurstan, it cost her all her strength to reach him, and she looks as if she has just had the hope crushed out of her."

"I'll tell you one thing," said Orm. "She's a high-born Norman. She's the kind who not only has brothers but a hall of household knights as well. So where are they, and why should you risk your neck for her if they won't?"

"You were there the day I made my vow of knighthood," I reminded him, but I was staring ahead with opened eyes. We had reached the eastern gate of the city, and Jordan cast a spray of coins from his wallet to the beggars squatting in the arch. Maud rode at his side with her back straight as a sword, as if she had been riding since she was a girl. Orm was right – only the rich and noble taught their daughters to ride.

"She needs help to get home," I said. "At least I know that."

"Aye," said Orm, "but you take care of yourself."

"I was hoping," I said, "that you might come with me."

The old Viking did not reply at once, but I knew he must be tempted, for Cumbria was his homeland even though he had left it before I was born. "I'll come," he said, and only then did he smile. "My brother Hoskuld will have rebuilt the hall at Longthwaite. The pillars will need carving."

"It will be good to go back," I said happily, though what I meant was that it was good to know Orm and Aimeric would be with me.

I gazed at Maud de Rumilly and wondered. By sealing her lips, Thurstan had locked us outside her sorrow. He had entrusted us with a small mysterious casket but kept the key to himself.

Even with Jordan at her side she looked alone, and as we rode through the slanting shadows of the Forest of Galtres, I felt as if we were invisible to her.

2. THE CASTLE OF THE PATRIARCH

Walter Espec, sheriff of Yorkshire and lord of Elmeslac, rose from his supper to greet us. We were dismounting in the bailey when he appeared in the doorway of the hall and roared my father's name, then strode down the steps, two at a time, to clasp Jordan in his arms.

Behind them, the doorway filled with people. Walter's sister came out bearing a jewelled chalice filled with wine. She offered it to Jordan, and as he raised it in salute to the faces in the doorway, they fell silent.

In that moment a halo of legend shone around Jordan and his men. They were returning from the very edge of the kingdom. They had held their castle against the Scots when all Northumberland had fallen and they had passed beyond the reach of help. The folk of Elmeslac had given them up for dead, and this was why it took them a moment to believe their eyes. It was only when Jordan set the chalice to his lips, and they saw his throat move and a trickle of wine run down his neck, that they burst into a cheer of welcome.

When I came face to face with Adele, we brushed each other's cheeks in a formal kiss, but she laid her hand a moment on my shoulder with a grip like a hawk on a fist. Her dark beauty had always run deepest after dusk, and her honey-brown eyes were full of joy.

"This is the answer to our prayers," she said, gazing at Jordan and his men. "It came in time."

"Peace?" I asked. "It came in time, but we will have to pay for it."

"How?" asked Adele.

"The Scots keep Northumberland and Cumbria."

"Then call me selfish," said Adele, "for all that matters to me is that you are home." She saw the hesitation in my face and frowned. "Have I spoken too soon?" she asked. "I was hoping you had come to stay the winter."

"I will," I promised, "but there is a short journey I have to make first."

I looked round for Maud and saw she was being embraced by the lady Albrea and her daughters. Adele followed the line of my gaze.

"Who is she?" she asked.

"That," I replied, "is what I am counting on you to find out."

In the torchlit and tapestried hall, the lady Albrea gathered the women to one end of the high-table to let Walter sit among his warriors like King Arthur with his knights. It was over a year since Walter and Jordan had supped together, and they had so many stories to tell that I was spared having to tell mine.

When the women rose to withdraw, Adele took her chance to pause and whisper in my ear as she went by. "Maud wants to visit the monks who fled from Calder," she said. "I have told her we will take her tomorrow."

Adele led us through the woods of Ryedale and by sunken lanes up onto hills where the fields were green with shoots of winter wheat.

"We are no longer on my father's land," she told Maud. "All this belongs to Roger de Mowbray."

Maud gave a nod but made no reply. She still looked tired and locked in her own thoughts.

"It is Roger," said Adele, "who has given the monks from Calder a refuge. He has promised them a manor, but for the moment they are living at a hermitage below the cliffs on the road to Thirsk."

"I am hoping," Maud said stiffly, "that they will return home with me."

"Were they your neighbours in Cumbria?" I asked.

"Calder Abbey stood on my land," she replied. "My brother Ranulf was its founder."

"How did it come to be burned?" asked Adele. "I thought King David gave abbeys the right of sanctuary?"

"He did," I said, "but the war in Cumbria was waged by his nephew, William FitzDuncan, and FitzDuncan does not use knights for his work. He takes wild men from the hills of Galloway and turns them loose like packs of wolves to do his hunting for him."

"You speak as if you know him," said Maud.

"Aimeric and I once crossed his path," I said. "He picked us up as if we were thorns in his leggings and threw us into his dungeon even though he knew we served Thurstan and the Church."

Maud looked at me curiously, but said nothing.

"Roger would not be sad if the monks returned home," said Adele. "I have a suspicion he would sooner keep the manor for himself."

"When did you last see him?" I asked.

"I never go to Thirsk these days," Adele said quickly, but she blushed. "Roger still comes to Elmeslac, and we ride hawking, but he comes less and less." She turned to Maud to explain. "There was a time when I thought I would marry Roger de Mowbray, but his mother set herself against it, and she won."

Maud looked at her with sudden sympathy. "Why?" she asked. "To me you would seem the perfect daughter- in-law."

Adele gave a wry smile. "Roger's mother dreams dynasties, and I am no use in such designs. My blood is too impure to be mingled with the house of Mowbray."

"Because you are a sheriff's daughter?" asked Maud.

"Because I am a bastard," said Adele. "I am a nothing. I will always have a place in the women's chamber at Elmeslac, but no inheritance. When my father dies, his land will pass to his sisters and their children. I will never have a dowry to make me worthy of Roger de Mowbray."

"You should have married Robert de Brus," I teased her. "He was landless when he asked for you, but he is lord of Annandale now."

"Why did your parents never marry?" asked Maud.

"I do not know," said Adele, "and there is no one to tell me. No one ever speaks of my mother."

"Not even your father?"

Adele shook her head. "Even he is ashamed."

"I wish I could remember their story," said Maud. "I was told it once by your grandmother."

Adele looked at her keenly. "My grandmother?" she asked.

"Agnes de Beauchamp," said Maud. "She is a neighbour of mine in Cumbria."

We had come to where the hills fell away in a drop like the underlip of a wave. Before us stretched the vast plain of York, a patchwork of field and forest and the serpent coils of rivers, and in the distance we could see Roger de Mowbray's castle of Thirsk.

Adele pointed to the foot of the hill. "Do you see the steading with pigs and a thatched barn?" she asked Maud. "That is where your monks now live."

"This is a visit I wish to make alone," said Maud. "Will you allow it?"

"We'll watch from here," I said, for from the brow we would see every yard of her ride to the hermitage, and there was no danger in it. There were no outlaws on Roger de Mowbray's land.

"I will be back within the hour," Maud said gratefully, and we watched her trot down the steep winding track that led to the plain.

"How strange," said Adele.

"What have you been able to find out?" I asked.

Adele looked confused. "About Maud?" she asked.

"Has she spoken of her family?"

"Her mother is Cecile de Rumilly," said Adele, "the lady of Skipton. Her father and brothers are dead, but she has two sisters, both of them married."

"Did she not speak of her husband?" I asked. "She wears a wedding-ring."

"No," Adele said thoughtfully. "Not once."

"What if we discover that he is a monster?" I asked. "What if she fled to Thurstan to beg him to grant her a divorce?"

Adele grinned. "If that were the way of it, he would not be sending her back. He would send her to a nunnery. That is where they hide broken wives."

We dismounted, and while I tethered the horses to graze, Adele settled herself on a flat white rock. It was too small for two, so I squatted at her feet, trying to work up the courage to make her the gift of the bracelets. The moment did not feel right. She was staring at the distant castle of

Thirsk, thinking of the man who might have been her husband if only her parents had married with the blessing of the Church.

It seemed uncanny to me how alike we were in our lives. We were both the bastard offspring of Norman knights, and just as Adele had found Roger but lost him, so it had been for me with Catriona. And in many ways I knew Adele more deeply than I had ever known Catriona. Our friendship was three years old, and it had never been broken.

"There is no shame in being a bastard," I told her. "It does not trouble me that my parents were too hungry for each other to wait for the blessing of the Church."

"It is different for you," replied Adele. "When you found your true father, it was the beginning of your road to knighthood. I was only told the day my mother died, and it was Aunt Albrea – not Father – who told me. I was nine years old. Until then I had been the princess of an enchanted castle, and my awakening was the truth that none of it belonged to me."

"When I win a domain," I said, "I will offer it to you."

Adele laughed and patted my neck as if I were a horse. "Bless you, Simon, for a most courteous reply, but I would hate you to marry me out of pity."

"It would not be with pity," I said. "It would be with longing."

That locked her eyes to mine, and there was sorcery in the beauty with which she looked at me then. "I believe you," she said, but then she shook her head. "No, you are saying all this to lift my spirits."

"If this were just courtesy," I asked, "would I have come prepared with a gift?" With the flourish of a juggler I pulled the bundle from my wallet and held it out to her like an offering to a saint. She untied it with quick fingers, and we both caught our breath as three silver bracelets shone in the sunlight.

"They are Moorish," I said, thankful to Orm but glad he was somewhere else, "one for each year of our friendship."

"They are exquisite," said Adele, kissing my cheek, "and I will treasure them." She looked down at the hermitage and laughed. "All in one day," she said. "I am rich."

"With me you may never be rich," I warned her.

She shook her head. "People are what I treasure," she said. "I have always felt your love, and you know all you are to me, but until today I never knew I had a grandmother still living."

"No one has ever told you?"

"Mother never spoke of her family," said Adele. "I do not even know where she came from. I know my father took her against her family's wishes, but that is all."

I imagined a young Walter Espec, less stout and his beard still jet-black, galloping away from a Cumbrian stronghold with a maiden like Adele riding at his side. "They must have been great days," I said enviously.

"If they were," said Adele, "why is my father too ashamed to speak of them?"

To my dismay I saw that Maud was already returning from the hermitage. She did not look as if her spirit had found solace; she looked crushed.

"That took no time," said Adele. "Are the monks no longer there?"

"They are there," said Maud, "and all they want is to be left in peace. I asked them to return to Calder, but they do not wish to come."

She rode on by, and Adele and I exchanged glances as we hurried to mount and follow.

"You are right about the monster," said Adele, "but it is not her husband. She looks like someone who is struggling all alone against evil."

"That would explain why she turned to Thurstan," I agreed, "and why I have a feeling she asked for more than he could give."

"She certainly looks to me as if she is losing the struggle," said Adele.

When we rode into Elmeslac, Arnoul and Hemming were waiting for me in the bailey.

"A messenger has come from York," said Arnoul. "Thurstan has summoned you."

"We must leave at once," said Maud.

"We cannot reach the city by dusk," I told her, "but I promise we will leave at daybreak."

Adele ushered Maud into the hall. Arnoul and Hemming came with me to stable the horses, each looking as if he were waiting for the other to speak.

"Was there more to the message?" I asked.

Arnoul shook his head. "We were thinking that now you are a knight, you need a squire. I would be proud to be your squire."

"And a groom," said Hemming. "A knight must have his own groom."

I laughed gratefully. They were the only two of Jordan's men who were my own age, and we had fought side by side in Northumberland. I knew their worth.

"If all goes well it will be no great adventure," I warned them, "and the nature of the task means that if we meet trouble we may have to run from it rather than fight it – but if what you want is a long ride to feel the wind after a year under siege, then come."

We were rubbing down the horses when the tall figure of Walter Espec entered the stables, and Jordan with him.

"Before you leave, Simon," said Walter, "I want you to choose yourself a horse fit for a knight."

I was sad to even think of forsaking my shaggy old Loki, but it was true that on one of Walter's thoroughbreds I would cut a finer figure. I chose a chestnut hackney named Caspar that I had ridden before, and as I turned to thank the lord of Elmeslac, I saw him ordering Arnoul and Hemming out of earshot. Walter looked down at me with a frown of long-bristled eyebrows.

"Have you been wooing my daughter?" he asked. "She has just begged me to let her ride with you to Cumbria."

I gazed back defiantly. "I love Adele with all my heart," I said, "but that will not be why she asked. She has just learnt that her grandmother is Maud's neighbour."

"Christ in glory!" muttered Walter. "Is the ogress still alive?" He studied my face, and I could tell he was wondering how much I knew. "No," he said, "I cannot allow it."

"I will protect her with my life," I promised.

"I know you would," said Walter, "but this is winter, not the season of pilgrimages, and you will have more than enough on your hands without my daughter."

"Thurstan would not be sending us unless the road were safe," I countered.

"If the road were safe," said Walter, "Thurstan would not be sending our best young knight as Maud's escort. Do not fool yourself, Simon. Once you cross the Stainmoor into Cumbria, you pass beyond our reach. We can offer a ransom to have you back, but no more. We cannot come to your aid with force without being accused of breaking the peace treaty before it is signed."

Jordan had been listening uneasily. "Even though Thurstan gave this task to you and not to me," he said, "perhaps I will ride with you."

"No," Walter told him, "I need you here."

"I will have Orm," I said, "and Arnoul and Hemming. I will be in good company."

Walter still looked troubled. "When you were last in Cumbria," he said, "you came up against William Fitz-Duncan. How did you part? Is there still a quarrel between you?"

"Aimeric and I were nothing to him," I said. "I doubt he even remembers us."

"I'll pray you're right," said Walter grimly.

"Believe me, my lord," I told him. "I will do all in my power to never again set eyes on William FitzDuncan."

"That may be harder than you think," said Walter. "Maud de Rumilly is his sister-in-law. To take her home, you must cross his domain."

3. THE UNBIDDEN ANGEL

A s we rode through the Forest of Galtres, I turned to Maud with the questions that had gnawed at me in the night.

"Yesterday we spoke of William FitzDuncan," I reminded her, "but you did not say if you knew him yourself."

"I know him," said Maud, and her voice had no love in it. "He is my brother-in-law."

"Then why did his men burn the abbey at Calder?" I asked. "Why did he strike the lands of his own kith and kin?"

Maud looked away. "I cannot talk of this."

It was the answer I had been dreading, for if she could not talk of it, then it must be what Thurstan had forbidden her to tell, and the force of evil that had driven her to him was William FitzDuncan.

Sitting beside Thurstan was a man my father's age, with reddish skin and a chin that stuck out over robes that were not the green and gold of a prelate but the stark black and white of a canon of the Augustinian rule. A balding brow had broken the ring of his tonsure, and he was packing documents into a satchel as Maud and Aimeric and I were ushered into the archbishop's chamber.

"Aethelwold is my right hand," Thurstan told us. "He has been kept from his flock by the war, but now at last he is returning to Caerluel. You will be his escort, and he yours. From Caerluel it is a day's ride to Maud's castle of Egremont, and you will set out only when Aethelwold judges it safe for you to go."

"Is William FitzDuncan still the lord of Caerluel?" I asked.

"No," said Bishop Aethelwold, with evident relief. "King David has sent Hugh de Morville to restore peace and law to Cumbria – but FitzDuncan is still the lord of Rath Sanas in Allerdale. To reach Egremont, you must cross his domain."

"Do I have reason to fear him?" I asked.

"Always," said Bishop Aethelwold.

"Indeed," said Thurstan, "which is why you must let Aethelwold choose the moment for the last stride of your journey."

"Will FitzDuncan be against it?" I asked.

Thurstan considered a moment, and I knew when he spoke that he had been debating whether to tell me more. "I want you to have no quarrel with him," he said. "If you meet, I want your ignorance of all but your task to shine in your eyes. The less you know, the clearer will be your wits."

"So my task ends when Maud is safe in Egremont?"

"No," said Thurstan. "Stay the night there, however cold your welcome, and in the morning ask Maud if she will return with you. If she is willing, bring her safely back to me."

Maud was shaking her head. She had been staring out of the window at the towers and roofs of the minster, with a look on her face as if all we were saying was so far from what she had hoped for when she came to Thurstan as to be meaningless.

"Close to Egremont," Thurstan told Aimeric, "you will find Saint Bega's Priory. It is an ancient house, lost to desolation until Maud's father restored it with monks from Saint Mary's here in York. I want you to take the prior a gift of food and mules, as well as letters that Aethelwold will give you."

The old archbishop sat back in his chair. His legs were shaking with palsy, and he looked tired beyond tiredness.

"Whatever you see and whatever you learn," he said, "remember all that hangs in the balance. It has been agreed that the treaty of peace shall be signed in Durham, but I have failed to persuade King Stephen to honour the signing with his presence. Queen Maud will be there in his place, to bestow the earldoms of Northumberland and Cumbria on Prince Henry of the Scots in return for his oath of loyalty. I had been hoping to bring it about by Christmas, but I now fear we must wait until Easter. Already there are barons close to the king who speak against it, so we must pray for the truce to hold. There must be no bloodshed this winter, or all could yet be lost."

I had an odd feeling that by the end of the speech he was talking less to Aimeric and me than to Maud.

"What are we to do," I asked, "if Maud does not wish to return to York with us?"

"Bring yourselves home," said Thurstan, "by the straightest roads."

We were to leave at daybreak, so Thurstan gave us lodging in the hostel on the staith.

Maud bid us goodnight as soon as supper was finished

and climbed to the loft, where we had rigged a hanging to make her a chamber. I told Arnoul and Hemming they could run wild in the city. When they had gone, Orm and I settled ourselves on a bench with two cups of mead, our belts unbuckled and our feet on the hearthstone.

"How long is it since we rode to Cumbria?" he asked.

"Three years," I said. "It was the first journey I ever made with you and Jordan."

Orm grinned. "I remember that you were so stricken with longing for my niece that I had to warn you to keep your distance."

"Sigrid the golden-haired," I said ruefully. "She was my first encounter with the witchcraft of love."

"Is that why you returned?" asked Orm. "Because it was Sigrid who cried for help?"

"She was crying for *you*," I said, "but you were a week's ride away in Northumberland."

"So you set out there and then with Aimeric," said Orm. "I'll bet he had no idea what he was riding into."

I stared unhappily into my cup. "When we came to Longthwaite, we found the hall burned down, Thord dead and Hoskuld and Arni carried off. It was the work of men from Galloway. Aimeric and I rode to Caerluel because we believed King David would have a sheriff there. Instead we found FitzDuncan with men from Galloway all around him. He had us thrown into the dungeons."

"Is that when you found Hoskuld and Arni?" asked Orm.

"We were thrown into separate holes," I said. "Aimeric found himself sharing a dungeon with several others. Hoskuld and Arni were among them."

"While you found yourself sharing a cell with Catriona," said Orm merrily. "How long were you in there?"

"A lifetime," I said, and my hand shook as I raised my cup to my lips.

The smile vanished from Orm's face. "So it was FitzDuncan who sent the raiders who burned Longthwaite and killed my nephew?" he asked. "You are sure of it?"

"It was FitzDuncan," I said balefully.

Orm spat into the embers of the hearthstone. "It is a great pity he is King David's nephew," he said. "We cannot kill him without breaking the truce – but if I ever find the men who did his bidding, I'll make them wish they had chosen to be monks."

"Most of them died in the Battle of the Standard," I said.

"I hope they did," said Orm, "for their sakes."

We were lost in separate broodings when there was a sound of hooves on the cobbled staith, and they came to a halt at our door. I rose and went to open it, and had to raise a hand to shield my eyes from the yellow light of a lantern that was being waved in my face by one of the porters from the archbishop's palace.

He spoke to a figure on horseback behind him. I heard a chink of coins, then the man with the lantern was on his way, leaving me to peer up at the rider, a shape cut out of darkness and silver-edged by moonlight, with long hair bound at the back of her neck in a plait.

"Catriona!" I said joyfully.

"Should I be?" asked Adele, and as soon as she spoke I recognised her by her horse, her riding-boots and her bearing. It was Adele, and it could never have been anyone else. I gave a groan and stepped forward to grasp her stirrup.

Adele dismounted and kissed me on the cheeks. Hers were cold. "Are you disappointed?" she asked.

"No," I protested, "but why are you here?"

"To ride with you to Cumbria," said Adele. "Why else?"

With a whisk of her cloak she walked past me into the hostel. Orm stood and offered her his chair.

"Adele is riding with us," I told him.

Orm gave her a grin. "You'll not regret it," he told her. "Cumbria is a fine land. I'll see your horse to the stable." He stepped outside, closing the door, and I hurried to pour Adele a cup of wine.

"You must be hungry," I said. "We have bread, ham, and there is even a crust of the apple and bramble tart."

"In a moment," said Adele. I turned with the wine and felt her eyes searching my face. "Are you waiting for her?" she asked.

"Who?" I asked.

"The woman whose name you spoke."

"It was chance," I said. "We were talking of her as you rode up."

"You spoke her name as if it were life itself."

"It is," I said, and I felt like a man accused of heresy declaring his faith.

Adele gave me a long frown, then she took the cup of wine and stared into it before she drank.

"You are the one," I reminded her, "who first told me of the witchcraft of love, of how many spells of desire we find ourselves bound by. I have never told you of Catriona because when I am in Elmeslac with you, she is not even in my mind."

"But she is when you are in York?" asked Adele.

"We parted in the summer," I said. "She left me at the gates of Tynemouth Priory and vanished into the war. I do not even know where she is."

"But are you waiting for her?" Adele asked again.

"No," I said. "Remember all I said to you yesterday."

"I have not forgotten," Adele assured me.

"So how did you bring Walter to change his mind?" I asked, steering the talk to what I hoped would be calmer currents.

"I did not even try," Adele confessed. "Father and Jordan set out for Whitby on sheriff's work. They will be gone three days. I told Aunt Albrea I was riding to visit Roger in Thirsk, and here I am."

"Did no one see you take the road to York?" I asked.

"I rode to Thirsk. Roger sent two of his men to escort me to the city gates. He also sends you his greeting."

"I have a feeling," I said, "that your father may be none too happy about this."

"By the time he finds out," said Adele, "we will be in Cumbria. When we return he will be too pleased to have us back to be angry."

I was none so sure, but I had never seen Adele so illuminated by a sense of purpose, and it did not make it easy for me to think for myself.

"Out of loyalty to your father," I said, "I should take you straight back to Elmeslac."

"Is that what you want to do?" she asked.

"No," I said, "but I am only a knight, and you are asking me to go against the will of my lord."

Adele looked at me with an intensity that made me hold my breath. "I am asking you to take me to my grandmother," she said. "I have to meet her. I need to hear my mother's story from her lips. I want to ride with you – but if you will not take me, Simon, I swear I will go alone."

She flung those last words at me like a challenge, and I knew that all we would ever be to each other hung on the answer I gave. It was as if she were telling me to choose. I could be her man, or her father's, but not both.

"I must know why my parents never married," said Adele. "I must know if I am under a curse. Do you understand?"

"No," I said, "but I believe you."

"Then you will take me?"

"I will be proud to be your escort." I clinked my cup against hers and raised it in salute, and suddenly it was Adele who looked hesitant. "Now you must eat," I told her.

Orm came in and set Adele's saddle-bag on the table. "Clear and cold," he announced, "the best weather we could have."

When Adele had eaten her way through everything we set in front of her, we lit her a lamp and showed her the way to the loft. Maud awoke, and we heard a flutter of talk above us in the eaves.

Orm spread our sheepskins beside the hearth and rolled himself contentedly in his cloak. "I hope I'm not going to be woken by the ladder to the loft creaking in the middle of the night," he warned me.

"You've taken her coming very quietly," I said. "I expected you to have more to say about it."

He opened one eye and winked it at me. "The way I see it," he said, "the more women and priests we have with us, the less FitzDuncan can claim that he mistook us for a band of outlaws."

4. THE WIZARD'S GREETING

W e left York at dawn, and I was impressed by the length of our cavalcade when it stretched into line along the frosted road. As well as the canons and servants of the bishop's household there was a train of two dozen mules, their baskets piled high and covered with waxed cloth lashed over with twine.

"I thought they were supposed to be making the road safe for us?" asked Orm. "When you can count more mules than horsemen, you know the horsemen are worth robbing."

I told Arnoul and Hemming to ride at the tail, and I rode with Orm at the head of the cavalcade. In Ripon, where we slept our first night, they told us there were outlaw bands in the Forest of Marwood, but we saw nothing to trouble us until we came to land that had been scoured by the war.

Where the road turned west into the wide vale below the Stainmoor, we entered a cattle country that had been stripped of its cattle, and came to villages that were no more than charred gable-ends. I had seen it in so many other places that I should have been hardened to it, but I saw the desolation mirrored in the eyes of Adele.

"Who could be so cruel?" she asked. "How could anyone do this?"

"It is the work of a man named William FitzDuncan," I said, glancing at Maud. "He came over the Stainmoor with a host drawn from Galloway. This was their path."

"I trust they will not go unpunished," said Adele, with all the outrage of a sheriff's daughter and such innocence that Maud smiled.

"Most of them fell in the Battle of the Standard," I said. "Those who escaped came back this way in a hurry, riding for their lives."

"Rich enough to keep them content – for a while," said Maud bitterly.

"You say that as if you think we were wrong to make peace," I told her.

"The truth is that I am jealous," said Maud. "You have bought yourselves peace. I belong to the lost domains of Cumbria and Northumberland who will pay for it."

"What would you have us do," I asked, "fight over who should rule until there is no land left to rule?"

"I can see you lack the spirit for it," said Maud.

"My father fought for Northumberland when everyone else had thrown open their gates," I retorted. "Never accuse –"

"Simon!" protested Adele, warning me with her eyes that I was breaking the bounds of courtesy.

I begged Maud's pardon, and she begged mine, but the fact remained that for a moment Maud had looked at me as if I were the cause of her misfortune, and that moment was enough to give me a glimpse of the root of her grievance.

I heeled Caspar forward and rejoined Orm at the head of the cavalcade. "A lost domain," I told him, "is what lies at the heart of all this. I have a feeling that when the treaty is signed and sealed and law, Maud de Rumilly will lose her land."

* * *

On the bare brown heights of the Stainmoor, we came to the gate of Cumbria.

It was no more than a tall stone cross that stood alone in the middle of the wilderness, bearing witness to the invisible line that kings had drawn with the tips of their blades along the watersheds of the flat-topped hills to north and south. The treaty would do no more than set in writing what we all knew, that to pass the cross was to leave King Stephen's realm and enter the domain of King David of the Scots.

For me, it was the place where I left my own land and entered William FitzDuncan's, and the threshold where I led Adele beyond her father's reach. I touched the carved stone shaft of the cross as I rode by. Beyond, the gate swung wide and we saw the deep Vale of Eden stretching like the bailey of a giant's castle towards a distant keep-tower of high domed fells.

Orm's gaze went out to the fells in greeting. "I'm glad I came," he said.

"So am I," I told him, for as the road tilted down into the Vale of Eden, I felt the gate swing shut behind us.

We slept the night in Appleby, and in the morning were on our way before the mists had cleared. By noon we were north of the Lake Fells and at the rim of the world I knew, on the old straight road that led through the Forest of Inglewood to the red stone ramparts of Caerluel.

For the last mile, Orm and I fell back to let Bishop Aethelwold lead the way, for this was his hour of triumph. He was returning to the city which the war had left him wondering if he would ever see again, and he gazed at it as though it were Jerusalem.

Caerluel received him with ceremony. No sooner had

we dismounted at Saint Mary's Priory than we were kneeling in the church as the canons raised their even chant in thanks, prayer and praise; and then, along a street where a crowd had gathered for the bishop's blessing, we rode from the priory to the castle. Waiting in the great hall was Hugh de Morville, the lord constable of Scotland. He knelt at the bishop's feet, then rose and kissed Aethelwold on the cheeks.

"Welcome in the name of King David," he greeted us, and we stood with bowed heads while the bishop prayed for wisdom, peace and prosperity.

De Morville gave me a smile of recognition, for we had met at King David's court before the war, but I found myself lost for words. I was staring at the woman who stood at his shoulder. It was as if a wizard had taken Adele and conjured her into a woman twenty years older. The brown eyes, the tall nose and brow, the turn of the lips, all were the same. De Morville noted the look on my face with amusement; he must have thought I had been stricken by longing.

"My wife," he said, "the lady Beatrice de Beauchamp."

I bowed and turned to beckon Adele, but she was already at my side and dipping shyly in a curtsey. The lady Beatrice gazed as if she were looking at her own ghost.

"What is your name, child?" she asked.

"Adele Espec, my lady, or Adele de Beauchamp. I am your niece."

"You are Adeline the day I last saw her," the lady Beatrice exclaimed. "No one else could be your mother."

Amidst a chorus of exclamations, Adele was embraced by her aunt and uncle and surrounded by cousins she had never known she possessed. At first she kept catching my eye to share her joy, then they engulfed her, and I felt as if she had been snatched from me in the middle of a harvest-dance.

To Maud de Rumilly they gave a cooler welcome. Hugh de Morville seemed embarrassed by her presence, and when we took our places for supper, the steward led her to one of the lower tables. I was offered a place of honour beside Bishop Aethelwold, but I judged it my duty to sit with Maud. Adele had no need of me; she would be well cared for by her long-lost kith and kin.

Orm had kept with Maud, as had Arnoul and Hemming. Once I joined them, we made a shield-ring around her, and she looked at us gratefully.

"One more day, then you will be free of me," she said with a smile, but it faded from her face as she caught sight of a man who had just entered the hall and was pulling off his gloves as he strode towards the high-table. He was nodding to left and right, calling out greetings, and when his eyes fell on Maud he grinned like a demon and bowed as he went by.

"Is that him?" Orm asked me.

"Yes," I said numbly.

I watched as William FitzDuncan took the place at the high-table that had been laid for me. He had come through the war without even a scar. The only change in him was that he had let his hair grow long, and together with his thick moustache it gave him the look of a warrior in an ancient carving.

Bishop Aethelwold greeted him with what looked like a sermon urging repentance. FitzDuncan listened tolerantly; he made some reply, and Hugh de Morville laughed. I knew then that even though he might no longer be running wild, FitzDuncan was still among friends. It was Maud who was the outsider.

"Tomorrow I ride to Egremont," she declared, "whatever Bishop Aethelwold may advise."

"He may be asking for our safe-conduct at this very

moment," I replied. "Now FitzDuncan knows we are here, it makes little difference. Is it a long journey to your castle?"

"It can be done in winter daylight," said Maud. "You will be back here by sunset on the day after tomorrow."

"Thurstan is praying that you will be with us," I reminded her.

"God alone knows what I will do," Maud said quietly.

"I know what it is to be helpless against FitzDuncan," I told her. "He had me thrown into the cellars beneath this hall, and he left me there for fifteen weeks."

"How did you endure it?" asked Maud.

"I was never alone," I said. "How do you endure?"

"I am beginning to fray," she replied, but then she shook her head, warning me to ask no more.

The meal was barely over when FitzDuncan rose from the high-table and sauntered towards us.

"How is my fair sister-in-law?" he asked. Maud gave him a look that could have withered a field of corn, and he relished it. "The good bishop asks me to grant you safe-conduct through Allerdale," he said. "I told him I would be honoured to take you to Egremont myself."

"If he suggests I accept your offer," replied Maud, "I will tell him that I would sooner crawl blind through a pit of vipers."

FitzDuncan laughed, and his gaze fell on me. "You have my safe-conduct to come and go," he told Maud. "All I ask in return is a moment's talk with your noble escort."

He gave an edge of irony to his last two words that made me wince, but I did my best to smile. "We have met before, my lord," I reminded him.

"Indeed," said FitzDuncan. "It is what I wish to talk about. We need privacy. One of the upper chambers should suit our purpose."

I rose to my feet, aware not only of Maud's and Orm's unease but of Aimeric watching me from the high-table. FitzDuncan walked to a doorway in the walls of the keep, took a torch from its bracket, and by its light we climbed a narrow stairway. I trotted at his heels, all my thoughts on keeping my footing.

"How is my little Catriona?" he asked. "Or have you tired of her?"

"You will never find her," I said. "She is free of you."

"Until the day I find her begging at my gate," he said. "She was no use to me once she grew into a mind of her own. You did me a service in ridding me of her."

We had reached the top of the stairs, where Fitz-Duncan opened a door and stood back to let me be the first to go through. I stepped out into darkness and damp night air to find slippery planks beneath my feet. I was on the palisaded walkway that ran around the roof of the keep. FitzDuncan lodged the torch in a bracket inside the doorway and stepped out to join me.

Clouds hid the stars and muffled the city in darkness. I could not even see the rooftops, and it felt as if we were alone on a pinnacle in hell.

"So tell me," said FitzDuncan, "did you find it?"

"Find what, my lord?" I asked, knowing full well.

"The Sacred Blade," he said. "Do not deny that you were searching for it. I have abandoned my own search, so you risk nothing by telling me the truth."

"We found it," I said proudly. "Thurstan has laid it in a place of safe-keeping where it will rest until the end of time."

"Tell me how it looks," he said.

"That, my lord, you will never know."

FitzDuncan laughed. "Well done, Simon de Falaise,"

he said. "You join the lucky few who have cheated me and lived. But the war is over, and neither of us can claim to have won all we fought for. How has Thurstan rewarded you? Meanly, I imagine, with blessings and fine words on the quest of knighthood. You will never prosper in his service – but I have a task that needs your skills, and if you serve me I will give you something better than the promise of heaven, which is all you will ever get from Thurstan."

The irony had left his voice. He said all this quietly and persuasively. I felt as if the keep-tower were spinning – I swayed and gripped the parapet to steady myself – but what had set me reeling was the thought of turning my back on all I was trying to be and throwing in my lot with William FitzDuncan. For a moment I let myself imagine the rewards.

"I already have a task," I said stiffly. "I doubt I can serve both you and Maud de Rumilly."

"There is nothing you can do to help her," said FitzDuncan. "Thurstan knows it, or he would not be sending her home empty-handed. I trust he told you not to meddle in her sorrows. Ours is a family quarrel, and you would be well-advised to keep out of it."

"Have we safe-conduct across your land?" I asked.

"At a price," said FitzDuncan. He lowered his voice even though there was no need and breathed his next words down my neck. "I want you to find me the Runes of Alnerdal."

"What are they?" I asked.

"Ancient," he said, "and hidden, but you have a gift for searching and you come to Cumbria with fresh eyes. You may see further than I can."

I shook my head. "I want nothing more to do with the secrets of the past."

"You will never escape their power," said Fitz-

Duncan. "Those who lived before us do not vanish. They are all around us, Simon, and I draw the men who serve me from both worlds."

He was staring out over the parapet as if he could see in the dark. I wondered if I were truly in the presence of a wizard, or if he were simply taking me for young and gullible.

"If I find you the Runes of Alnerdal," I said, "would you use them against Maud de Rumilly?"

"Forget her," FitzDuncan said impatiently. "She is nothing."

There, I realised, was the measure of the distance between us. Maud was nothing to him. He could crush the bones of her life without even giving her a thought, for no better reason than that she stood in the way of his need or greed.

My hands strayed towards the knife at my belt. I thought of the lives past counting that had been lost in the war FitzDuncan had done more than any man alive to bring about. I had vowed only to kill for justice, and there would be justice in killing FitzDuncan.

"I can believe you talk with demons, my lord," I told him, "for that is what any man who serves you must become." Shivering with fear and revulsion, I stepped past him and walked to the torchlit doorway.

"All I am asking is the price of your safe-conduct," he called after me. "Take Maud to Egremont, then come to me in Rath Sanas. Who knows? By then you may be ready to beg for the chance to win my favour."

I gave no sign that I had heard, and groped my way down to the smoky light of the hall and the faces of my friends.

"Where is Maud?" I asked.

"She and Adele have gone with the women to their

chambers," said Aimeric. "She did not look happy when you left with FitzDuncan."

"What did he want?" asked Orm.

"He warned me not to meddle in a family quarrel," I said, "but we have his pledge of safe-conduct."

"How comforting," said Orm. "I wonder what it's worth."

"I'll tell you," I promised, "but only when Maud is safe in Egremont."

5. A SONG FOR TWO SISTERS

I woke from a bad dream and found I had rolled off my bedding, and I was still picking rushes and scraps from the hall floor out of my hair when Adele came to find me.

"Sablegarde is where my grandmother lives," she said. "My cousin Griselle says it is no distance at all from here, and that she will take me herself."

"Then I can leave with my mind at ease," I said. "It looks as if you do not need me."

Adele looked at me reproachfully. "You will be with me," she said. "Come as soon as Maud is safely home."

"Where is Maud?" I asked.

"She is ready to leave," said Adele. "She is waiting in the stables."

"Has she eaten?"

"She said she was not hungry." Adele lowered her voice. "Why is my aunt so cold with her?"

"Maud has a quarrel with William FitzDuncan," I said. "No one here wants to know of it, not even your good aunt and uncle, so they pretend not to see her."

"I will plead for her," said Adele.

"Let it be," I said. "They are bound by their loyalties.

FitzDuncan is King David's nephew, and Maud is only the daughter of a dead Norman lord." I looked over my shoulder, sure she must have walked into the hall and heard me. "Arnoul and Hemming will stay with you," I told Adele. "I cannot let Walter Espec's daughter ride to Sablegarde without an escort."

Adele gripped my shoulder and kissed me on the cheeks. "Promise me you will take every care," she said.

"Of Maud?" I asked.

"No," she said mischievously, "of Aimeric."

"I will bring him to you safely at Sablegarde," I promised her, "tomorrow at nightfall."

The look then in her gold-brown eyes was as potent as Thurstan's blessing, only richer, for it kept me warm as I walked out with Orm into the bailey, into rain spitting down from a swirling grey sky.

Maud greeted me with a curt nod. "FitzDuncan has granted us safe-conduct," I told her. "Does it surprise you?"

"Nothing he does would surprise me," she said. "What else did he tell you?" Her gaze was like an accusation, as if in talking to FitzDuncan I had betrayed her.

"We hardly spoke of you," I said. "We were raking over the embers of an old quarrel –"

"What did he say?" Maud persisted, and when I still hesitated, she glared at me. "You can tell me, Simon. I have learnt how to look truth in the face. I will not fall in a faint."

Even then I could not bring myself to look her in the eye. "He said that Thurstan is sending you home empty-handed, and he told me there is nothing I can do to help you."

Maud saw the misery in my face and touched me lightly on the arm. "I still need your help," she said, "even if it is only to ride home empty-handed."

We left Caerluel by the western gate, where the old straight road ran out into the Forest of Inglewood. We were a cavalcade of four, with trotting behind us the string of mules loaded with Thurstan's gifts for the monks of Saint Bega. Orm led them by tether. He was wearing a bright patterned woollen hat which gave his head the shape of an acorn, and he cursed like a mule-driver when we told him he looked like one.

The rain spat in our faces; we rode with hoods up and heads down for mile after mile. The forest gave way to pasture and ploughland, and through the drifting curtains of mist we saw manors and villages. The stillness of winter had settled on the fields. We seemed to be the only folk in Cumbria to have left a good hearth to brave the weather.

"Is this FitzDuncan's domain?" I asked Maud.

"It will be," she said. "He is waiting for his cousin to die. This is the first of the three domains of Allerdale; mine is the southernmost; FitzDuncan's lies between."

"So his cousin is lord here now?" I asked. "Where does he keep his stronghold?"

"He has no stronghold," said Maud. "His name is Alan Waltheofsson. When you return to Adele, I think she may tell you his story."

"It is sad?" asked Aimeric.

"The cruellest I know," said Maud, "and I could tell you some cruel tales of what we suffer for love."

"Would one of them be of your sister?" I asked.

Maud looked at me with surprise. "Of Alice?" she asked. "No. Alice set eyes on William FitzDuncan and knew there and then that she must have him whatever it brought in its wake. She chose her fate. She has all she wanted. A few more miles and you will see for yourself where he imprisons her."

The clouds were brightening, and the rain stopped as we were trotting down to a bridge over a wide river. We had almost reached it when the lifting clouds gave me a glimpse upstream to a tongue of high ground and the sharp outline of a palisaded stronghold, its walls green with lichen and rising above them the pointed roof of a hall. I barely had time to catch my breath and stare before the cloud rolled down and the castle was hidden. It was as if a huge malevolent eye had blinked open and then shut, content to brood in sleep now it knew where we were.

"Rath Sanas?" I asked.

"Rath Sanas," said Maud. To ride on was to feel the second invisible gate of our journey swing shut behind us, and here I almost heard the bars being dropped into their brackets. There was a man-at-arms waiting on the bridge to take our toll. He wanted a halfpenny for each of our mules, and even though it was naked brigandage we made no protest. Aimeric paid in bright silver coins from the mints of York and we hurried on through quiet villages onto a moor where Maud began to breathe the air as if it were holy.

The clouds had lifted to hang in the rafters of the sky, and we could see far and wide. Allerdale was not a dale but a great bench of land between the Lake Fells and the sea. Rivers cut across it, giving it valleys and hills, but they were overshadowed by the massive fells, whose flanks were now so close they felt like the wall of a darkened passage along which we were groping our way.

It was a passage lined with bones. On every side were scorch-marks that had once been villages. The fields had gone to waste; there was not an ox or pig or man to be seen, nor was there anywhere left where they would have looked at home. The land had forgotten them. This was not the work of the last year – when half Northumbria had gone up in flames – but of well before. The seasons were covering the ruins. War had not come here as a passing curse; it had settled to breed.

Maud kept her eyes on the road and her face a tight-lipped mask. Aimeric and I exchanged harrowed glances, but neither of us could find anything to say. We knew we had entered Maud's domain, and we had already seen enough to know it was a place to flee, not a place to return.

At the heart of the desolation stood the castle, its tall Norman keep-tower looking out over a land stripped bare. Here even the trees had been cut down. It was as if a dragon had come and blasted the land with fire, and the castle alone had endured.

"Egremont?" I asked.

"Egremont," said Maud, with more emotions in her voice than I could count. One of them was relief, as though she had been afraid the castle would no longer be there.

"A fine stronghold," I told her.

"My father built it to last a hundred years," said Maud. "It may yet."

She took a hunting-horn from her belt and blew a long clear note. No answering call came from the castle, but by the time we had climbed the track to its gates, they stood open. A figure on the ramparts shouted a greeting, and we gentled the horses across a rickety bridge that spanned a deep dry ditch to enter a gate-arch that was charred and black, as if the dragon had tried to burn his way in.

The lord of Egremont was waiting for us in the bailey, a tall man with grey hair who strode to grasp Maud's stirrup and catch her in an embrace before her feet had touched the ground. He looked old enough to be her father – or so I thought until I saw his face and realised with a shock that he was barely older than me.

We dismounted and bowed, and Maud named us to him.

"You are more than welcome," he told us. "I trust you are only the vanguard. I need men, not mules."

"They serve Thurstan," Maud said quickly. "They are the escort he has sent to bring me home. The mules are not even for us; they are for the monks of Saint Bega."

"And there is no one else?" he asked.

"No one," said Maud, despair in her face as the lord of Egremont turned away. She caught hold of his hand. "Richard," she said softly. "They have been kind. Please make them welcome."

He turned back and considered us, but I could tell we were nothing to him. It cost him an effort of will to stitch together the shreds of his courtesy.

"Ketel the steward will see to your every need," he told us. "We will meet again at supper."

As he led Maud towards the stairway of the keep-tower, a gnomelike old man with lute-peg yellow teeth stepped in front of me and bowed. I almost brushed him aside and hurried after Maud, but I remembered just in time that the journey was over. I was no longer Maud de Rumilly's guardian.

When she entered the hall that evening, Maud had shed her travelling-clothes for a close-cut gown of blue wool that deepened the colour of her eyes. Her pale hair had been brushed until it shone golden and wound into a single long plait. Richard of Egremont walked at her side, but the faces they greeted us with were bleached of any truth. It was as if they had made a vow of secrecy, a pact that we were to see and hear no evil, and leave Egremont no wiser than when we came.

Aimeric sensed it, and his talent for table-talk deserted him. The supper did little to add to our cheer: there was no wine, and our main dish was a mutton stew with a taste of stale spices. It was Richard who in the end gave way to impatience and began to question us about the treaty of peace. He wanted to know its terms down to the last compromise.

"King Stephen will never set his seal on such a disgrace," was his verdict when all was explained. "He can only have submitted to the truce to buy time. Once he has gathered an army from all England, he will come and take his revenge."

"I am afraid that seems unlikely," said Aimeric. "Half the barons of England are now in open revolt. Stephen has no choice but to let a part of his kingdom go. He needs both hands just to hold on to his crown."

"Surely you welcome an end to the war?" I asked Richard. "King David will be a better lord to Cumbria than Stephen has been, and all he will ask of you is that you swear an oath of loyalty to him or to his son."

"I doubt I would reach him alive," answered Richard, drawing his lips back and grinning like a skull.

I could not bear the look in his eyes, and turned to Maud, but she had risen and was talking with some of the women of the household. There were not many of them, and they were humbly dressed. Looking along the tables I counted only nine men who looked fit to bear arms. The hall had been built to hold ten times our number; we were huddled in the middle of it like children who had strayed into a forest.

Aimeric pointed to an object among the weapons and trophies that hung on the walls. "Is that a tambour?" he asked.

Ketel the steward reached up and lifted down a circle of taut hide stretched to fit a wooden hoop. "It is a bodhran," he replied, "from the days when Irish harpers used to come here."

Aimeric took the instrument and looked at it curiously. When he beat on it with the flat of his hand it gave a sound like a wing-beat. "I wish I knew an Irish song," he said, but he was already on his feet, beating a march on the drum of hide, and he broke into a song we all knew.

Ketel the steward began to stamp his foot to the beat, and soon we were all clapping or thumping the table, laughing with every twist of the old tale of knights outwitting the Pagans. I looked at the faces of the folk of Egremont. They were in another land, where their troubles were forgotten, and when Aimeric came flushed and breathless to the end of the song, they pounded the tables and begged for more. Orm had unwrapped Aimeric's lute and was holding it out to him, and he took it and began to tune the strings.

"Sing us a song of the troubadours," I called out, for they were the songs Aimeric sang best, when an echo of longing came into his voice that transfigured the cool chaste man of the Church with his tonsured hair and black cassock, and made him sing as if he were dressed in red, gold, and green.

"I will do better than that," he said. "I will sing you the first words of a new song – a song for Allerdale."

His fingers pecked the strings in ripples of notes like waves lapping on a shore. His eyes closed and his face set into a frown, and when the words came, he sang them as a lament, the firelight casting his shadow high on the smoke-blackened tapestries.

> *"Rowans red as blood*
> *guard the river by her gate,*
> *I curse her tower,*
> *her lord of hate,*
> *and pray for all*
> *imprisoned by their hearts."*

His hand rose from the strings, on his face a childlike joy at what he had found. I turned proudly to our hosts only to see Richard starting forward in his chair, his face and knuckles clenched, his expression one of shock turning to fury. Maud flew to his side and gripped his wrist.

"He is singing of Alice," she said quickly. "As we rode past Rath Sanas I told him her story."

Richard had lurched to his feet, but now he froze and gave us an idiot's grin. "They say an Irish harper will insult a man to his face," he said with a contrived laugh. "For a moment I thought that was your purpose. I'll bid you good night."

He turned and strode from the hall. My eyes met Maud's and she gave me a look as if she could gratefully have laid her head on my shoulder and wept. It lasted only a moment, then she gathered her wits, bid us goodnight and hurried after her lord.

Ketel the steward led us to a chamber in the galleries of the hall.

"What have I done?" Aimeric asked wretchedly as soon as we were alone.

"You're not to blame," said Orm. "It's not a fault when a song rings true to more than one heart."

Aimeric shook his head. "Did you see the look on his face? He wanted to kill me. From now on I will keep to Latin lyrics only churchmen can understand."

"Poor Maud," I said.

"She may not be as poor as you think," said Orm.

"What do you mean?" I asked.

"Richard must be the most valiant knight since William of Orange," he said. "I would like to know how he has held out against FitzDuncan for so long when he has barely enough men to guard the gates."

"However he has done it," I said, "he cannot last. He knows it; Maud knows it; all here know it. Maud has ridden home to her doom. What is worse is that FitzDuncan knows it. He told me himself that there is nothing we can do to help her."

"Aye," said Orm, "but he would say that, wouldn't he?"

Maud came to us soon after daybreak, when we were breakfasting in the hall. She was not dressed to ride, but to bid us farewell.

"Take Thurstan my thanks and my love," she said. "He will understand."

"Come with us," I said. "Leave this place of sorrow to the wolves."

Maud levelled her pale blue eyes on me. "Let me tell you what you must do, Simon," she said gravely. "Go to Adele and tell her that in my judgement you are a true knight, and she would be a fool not to marry you."

"Thank you," I said, flattered and blushing. "I will."

She swept us out to our horses as if she were aching to be rid of us. "To reach Saint Bega's Priory," she said, "you have only to cross the river and take the road towards the sea."

Looking up, I saw Richard outlined against the sky on top of the keep-tower. He raised his hand and I returned the salute, and it was of Richard – not Maud – that I was thinking as we rode with our string of mules through the charred archway onto the creaking bridge. He had a wife and castle I would have envied any man, but I would not have changed places with Richard of Egremont for all the gold in Christendom.

6. THE SECRETS OF ALLERDALE

ow we are alone," said Orm, "you can tell us what the widow-maker of Rath Sanas had to say for himself."

"FitzDuncan?" I asked. "He wanted to know if we had found the Sacred Blade, so I told him it was well out of his reach. Then he asked me to find him the Runes of Alnerdal."

"Runes of Alnerdal, eh?" said Orm. "Did he tell you what they are?"

"He said they are ancient and secret, and that someone who comes to Cumbria with a fresh eye may have the best chance of finding them."

"Runes are an old way of writing," said Aimeric. "No one uses them nowadays. All that needs to be written is written in Latin."

"Norse folk still use them," said Orm. "What answer did you give him?"

"I told him I have had enough of meddling with the secrets of the past."

"Very wise," said Orm, "and was that enough for him?"

I remembered the words FitzDuncan had called after me and felt as if he had taken a raven's shape and come swooping to perch on my shoulder. "He told me to go to him at Rath Sanas," I said. "He said it was the price of our safe-conduct."

Aimeric looked at me in horror. "And you agreed?"

"What would you have done?" I asked. "Challenged him to catch us if he could?"

"I take your point," said Aimeric, "but do you truly intend to go?"

Orm winked at me. "We can go tonight," he said. "It suits my purpose."

The joy had just been kicked out of Aimeric's morning. "God forgive me, I hate the man," he said miserably. "I hate him and all he embodies."

"Welcome to the brotherhood," said Orm.

We could already see Saint Bega's Priory. It stood at the mouth of a shallow valley, sheltered by a headland of red cliffs and lapped by a sea as grey as ash. Here at least there had been no burning: FitzDuncan had made his mark from a distance.

Huddled in the apple-garth and spilling out into the meadows were a jumble of log and turf bothies, crowded with folk who had fled their homes. They were the old, the widowed – and the children, who ran out to meet us when they saw the string of mules.

They chased us all the way to the priory gates with pleading outstretched hands, and the monks, alerted by the clamour, had to push them back and bar the gates in their faces before we could hear ourselves speak. The prior and all his brethren came out to welcome us, and became children themselves as they unloaded the panniers, praising Thurstan and the saints as among the sacks of grain they discovered spices and smoked hams, incense and candles.

The prior was a small man with dark eyes and a

furrowed face. He led us through the cloister to the chapter-house, where we sat in the light of misty glass windows and a novice brought us malt loaf and bilberry wine, to the torment of the prior's dog, who whimpered at our ankles and begged for scraps.

"As you can see," said the prior, "we have many mouths to feed. All you have brought is most welcome, but it will not go far."

"Bishop Aethelwold has returned to Caerluel," said Aimeric. "He will do all in his power to help."

"There will be famine," said the prior, "for as long as there is war."

"The war is over," said Aimeric, but as he explained the truce and the terms that were to be signed and sealed in Durham, the prior looked uncomforted.

"We have known for three weeks that something of the kind was under way," he said, "but it will not bring peace to Allerdale. There are men here locked in a quarrel that will end only when one or both of them lie dead."

"We know who you mean," said Aimeric.

"The lord of Rath Sanas and the lord of Egremont," said the prior. "I have never seen a hatred to match it."

"How did it begin?" asked Aimeric.

The prior spread his hands. "What are half the quarrels in the world about? About land, and who is to rule it."

"But surely FitzDuncan has no claim to Egremont?" I asked. "It belonged to Maud's father. She has it from him. Richard holds it by right of his wife."

"Ah, but that is just how FitzDuncan claims it," said the prior, "by right of *his* wife. He is married to Maud's sister. When a man dies, his domain passes whole to his eldest son, but if there are no sons, it is divided among his daughters. The law does not say how it must be divided, and that is where FitzDuncan makes his claim. Who can deny that his claim to Egremont is equal to Richard's?"

"How can you say that?" I protested.

The prior smiled and refilled our cups with bilberry wine. "I have watched this quarrel since the day it began," he said, "and it cannot be unravelled into right and wrong."

"So it is older than the war?" asked Aimeric.

"It goes back to the day FitzDuncan was given Rath Sanas," said the prior.

"Who gave it to him?" I asked.

"Waltheof his uncle," said the prior, "who was then the lord of Allerdale-below-Derwent. The lord of Egremont in those days was Maud's father, William Meschin. He and FitzDuncan took one look at each other and saw that each was everything the other hated. They never fought – FitzDuncan was a mere youth, and had not yet gathered his Galwegian angels of death – but they were never at peace."

"Then why did William Meschin let FitzDuncan have one of his daughters?" I asked.

The prior shook his head. "It could never have come about in his lifetime. It happened after his death, and it was the moment the quarrel burst into flame."

"Are you saying FitzDuncan married Alice out of hate?" I asked. "To make her suffer?"

"God forbid!" said the prior. "No, it was love, and for a while we thought it would save him. When William Meschin died, Egremont passed to Ranulf his son. Ranulf was the gentlest of men; I know, for I taught him his letters myself, here in our cloister. FitzDuncan set out to win Ranulf's friendship, and it was easily done. He came to Egremont, he set eyes on Alice, and the rest was the sorcery of desire."

"And that was more than Ranulf could bear?" asked Aimeric.

"Quite the opposite," said the prior. "He was enchanted. He thought his sister could have no better husband."

"So where was the quarrel?" asked Aimeric.

"With their mother, the lady Cecile de Rumilly. She fought against the marriage with all her strength. Ranulf stood with Alice, and Maud was torn in two."

"While FitzDuncan watched and fanned the flames?" asked Aimeric.

"Perhaps," said the prior, lowering his eyes. "It broke the family. When she had lost, the lady Cecile left for her castle of Skipton vowing never to return, and Maud went with her. All might have been well here, but Ranulf died young and, on the day he was buried, FitzDuncan claimed the domain of Allerdale-above-Derwent by right of his wife. He claims it was Ranulf's dying wish."

We were listening open-mouthed by now. The twists in the tale had taken us all by surprise.

"This was in the very season King Stephen took the crown of England," the prior went on. "FitzDuncan rushed to bring death to Northumberland in King David's name, and he was gone from Allerdale long enough for Cecile de Rumilly to hear of it and strike behind his back."

"She gave Egremont to Richard and Maud," I exclaimed.

"She sent them here with a force of knights drawn from King Stephen's own following," said the prior. "After that, there could be nothing but war. FitzDuncan's fury has known few bounds. This priory has been one of them, but there have been times when I have felt our fate hang by a thread."

"You told us you knew three weeks ago that peace was in the making," Aimeric said curiously. "What was the sign?"

"King Stephen recalled his knights," said the prior. "I knew then that he was abandoning Maud and Richard to their doom, and I fear it will not be long in coming."

"So what FitzDuncan seeks," I said, "is to be lord of all Allerdale?"

"Even if he takes Egremont he will not be that," said Aimeric. "His cousin Alan is still lord of Allerdale-below-Derwent."

"No, your friend is right," the prior told him. "Alan Waltheofsson is a broken man. He will never have children of his own. His land is already FitzDuncan's domain, and when FitzDuncan takes Egremont, he will be lord of Allerdale."

"You talk as if he cannot be stopped," I said.

"I can see no way to stop him, and believe me, I have searched," the prior replied. "I know him, but I do not understand him. He will come here to pray, losing himself in vigil and telling me later he saw Saint Bega herself in her coracle on the sea, and the next day he will order the burning of Calder Abbey because the monks have dared speak out against his deeds. He can see into the past and into the future, but his soul is lost and he gives his wisdom to evil. The only way those who block his path can be saved is by saving William FitzDuncan from himself – but I do not see how it can be done. I would not even know where to begin."

"So what will become of Richard and Maud?" I asked, but my voice was drowned by the tolling of a bell high in the church. The prior rose to his feet.

"The hour of Mass," he declared.

"And we must be on our way," said Aimeric.

"May God bring you safely home to York," the prior replied. He gave us his blessing and saw us out to the priory yard, slipping away through the cloister with his dog at his heels to leave us blinking in the sunlight, for the clouds had blown away and the sky was clear and cold.

"Let's go up on the headland," said Orm. "We'll not be here again, and I'd like a look out to sea."

We followed him up onto the cliff, where he gave a growl of pleasure.

"Look out there," he said. "The Isle of Manannan."

On the western edge of the world, twin blue hills rose from a sea no longer ashen but sparkling like crystal. They shimmered in the sky like a promise of a kingdom where hate was just a legend and love brought only happiness. We stood and gazed, wishing we were there and not in the lost domain of Allerdale-above-Derwent.

"Well," said Aimeric, "at least now my mind is at rest."

"At rest?" I echoed incredulously.

"What I mean," he explained, "is that we know now why Maud went to Thurstan. Once King Stephen had recalled his knights, Thurstan was her only hope. He was the man who when no one believed it could be done raised an army and won the Battle of the Standard —"

"But he could not give her knights to save Egremont without breaking the truce," I said with a groan.

"And we also know," said Aimeric, "why he forbade you to ask Maud what brought her to him."

"Do we?"

"Oh yes," said Aimeric. "Your vow of knighthood. He believes in you, Simon. It is the most beautiful compliment he could have paid you."

"How is it a compliment not to trust me?"

Aimeric smiled. "He must have reasoned that if you knew how utterly at FitzDuncan's mercy you were leaving Maud, you could not be trusted to ride obediently away."

"So it was to protect me?"

"To protect you from your vow," said Aimeric. "Orm and I are the only ones who know you know," he said quickly, "and we will never breathe a word."

"It is too late for that," I said. "It is what I know in my own heart that hurts."

"So what will you do?" asked Aimeric.

I turned to Orm. "What in hell *can* we do?" I asked.

He had turned from the sea to gaze inland. The last lingering clouds were blowing away in shreds, revealing the huge grey knuckles of the Lake Fells. I watched a smile spread over Orm's bearded face, as if he were greeting each fell by name.

"I'll tell you something," he said. "Alnerdal is the old Norse name for Allerdale. I'll tell you something else; I can read runes."

Aimeric looked as if he had been struck by a shaft of light from heaven. "Are you saying you can find the Runes of Alnerdal?" I asked.

"I'm saying it might not be a waste of time," replied Orm.

"But then what would we do?" I asked. "Take them to FitzDuncan and use them to bargain with?"

"One way or another we'd use them against him," said Orm. "When you know a man's desire, you know his weakness."

I gazed yearningly northwards. Somewhere in the invisible distance was the castle of Sablegarde. Orm and Aimeric said nothing. They were waiting for me to decide.

"I hate the pair of you," I told them, but they knew me well enough to know I was lying.

PART TWO
The Wizard's Domain

7. THE OGRESS

A dele has told me nothing of the day she came to Sablegarde. Most of what I know of it I have learnt from Griselle.

Griselle was in high spirits as she rode out of Caerluel with her new-found cousin. She was full of a secret design. Arnoul and Hemming were among the men-at-arms of their escort, and Arnoul remembers how when the land turned to barren marsh and they first caught sight of the castle, Adele looked round, fearfully, and when Arnoul caught her eye and grinned, she smiled with relief. So Adele was frightened on that last mile to her grandmother's gate.

As they reached Sablegarde, Griselle gave a signal to one of her men, who broke away from the cavalcade and rode on towards the dark sands of the estuary beyond.

Griselle led her cousin to the chamber where Agnes de Beauchamp spent her days brooding in solitude. Tapestries covered every crack in the walls and rugs every chink in the floor. The old lady rose to greet them, but instead of offering them her cheeks, she held out her hand for them to bend and kiss.

She gave Adele one deep, darting glance, then turned her stare on Griselle. "How many times must I ask you to send a herald to warn me of your visits?" she asked.

"Today, there was no time," said Griselle. "Look who I bring with me."

To greet her long-lost grandchild, Agnes de Beauchamp breathed in and straightened her back, even with the stoop of age matching Adele height for height. When she spoke, the words came out like sweeps of a scythe. "Why have you come?" she asked. "There is no inheritance for you here."

Both girls flinched. Griselle was no stranger to the bite of her grandmother's tongue, but she had never known her so cruel, smiling faintly as if seeing her words strike deep had given her pleasure.

Adele flushed crimson, but she replied with a level voice. "When I learnt you were my grandmother, it seemed only courteous to come and pay my respects. I learnt by chance, and I can see now why my father has never thought it worth telling me."

Griselle held her breath, waiting for her grandmother to retaliate, but the old lady confined herself to an icy nod of approval. "Very wise of him," she said. "I never speak of him either. I doubt he encouraged you to come, so why are you here?"

"I came for myself," said Adele. "I want to know the memories I bring you."

The old lady shook her head. "You ask too much," she said. "Go back where you came from. Leave the past in the past."

Adele looked crushed. At that moment they were joined by the lord and lady of Sablegarde, and Agnes de Beauchamp withdrew into silence. Even at supper, with her grand-daughters seated beside her, she behaved as if Adele were not there.

"What of this infamous treaty?" she asked Griselle. "Has it been sealed?"

Griselle knew nothing about it.

"You are a disgrace," her grandmother told her. "Your father is constable of Scotland. What do you talk of every night at his table?"

"The peace is to be sealed at Easter, in Durham," Adele said quickly, "by Prince Henry for the Scots and Queen Maud for the English."

Agnes de Beauchamp acted for a moment as if she had not heard, but her curiosity was too strong for her. "Do you happen to know how much of his kingdom that fool Stephen is surrendering to the Scots?" she asked.

Adele answered in such detail, naming the borders from Furness to the Tyne, that her grandmother was forced not only to look at her, but to look at her with undisguised interest. "Are you certain?" she asked. "Is Stephen truly throwing Furness into the bargain?"

"I think I have it right," said Adele. "The friends with whom I rode to Caerluel were in Rocksburgh the night the terms were agreed by King David."

"And what does your father make of it?" asked Agnes de Beauchamp.

"He says it is the price of peace."

"And how long does he think it will last?"

Adele lowered her voice. "He says it will last until a stronger man than Stephen wears the crown of England, but no longer."

Her grandmother asked no more questions, but when at the end of the meal she rose to retire, she rested her hand a moment on Adele's shoulder.

"You've more wits than your mother," she said, "but as to your looks, you're her beauty run coarse. If you still wish, you may attend me in my chamber in the morning before you leave."

The lord and lady of Sablegarde led the girls to their own chamber, where a bed had been prepared for them. In the light of a butter-lamp, the two cousins sat on the coverlet, unplaiting and brushing each other's hair.

"You were magnificent," whispered Griselle. "You won her over completely."

Adele shook her head and tears welled in her eyes.

"What is it?" asked Griselle. "How did you expect her to be?"

"Like my mother," said Adele, as she blew out the lamp.

In the morning, Adele ventured back to her grandmother's chamber.

"How did you reach Caerluel?" the old lady asked her.

"I rode with Simon de Falaise," said Adele. "You may have heard of him."

"I have heard of his father," said her grandmother, "but I did not notice a knight among your escort."

"He is in Egremont," replied Adele.

"What in the world has taken him there?"

"Maud de Rumilly. Archbishop Thurstan entrusted him with the task of escorting her home."

"Then I hope for your sake that he does not linger," said the old lady. "Have you given yourself to him?"

Adele blanched. "How could I?"

"Quite easily, I expect," said her grandmother, "if you were wild enough to go against your father's will to follow him."

Adele shook her head. "This is why I came to you. This is what I must know."

Agnes de Beauchamp looked at her piercingly. "What must you know?"

Adele sat forward, staring at the three silver bracelets on her wrist. "Since the day Mother died," she said, "Father has never once spoken her name. It is as if he were ashamed."

"Of you?"

"No," said Adele. "He treats me like a princess. It is what I am in the eyes of the world that frightens me. I have lost one man I loved because I am a bastard and could bring him no inheritance if we married. It made me feel unclean, as if I were a leper."

"You should be saying all this to your father, not to me," said Agnes de Beauchamp.

"No," said Adele. "You are the only one who will tell me honestly if I deserve it – because that is what I must know. Is this God's justice? Is it His judgement on the sins of my parents?"

"Why should you care about their sins?" asked her grandmother.

Adele drew off her bracelets and turned them in her hands. "What I must know," she said, "is if I am fit to ask the blessing of God and marry – or if I am damned, with a curse that if I marry I will pass to my children?"

"Child," said her grandmother, "the only sins your –"

She was interrupted by the entrance of a man Adele knew only as the lord who had come sauntering into the hall of the castle of Caerluel two nights before. He wore the same loose embroidered surcoat, gathered at the waist by a belt with a buckle of carved bone.

"Saint Kentigern's long life to you," he greeted Agnes de Beauchamp. "I was riding by and seized the chance to kneel at the altar of your wisdom."

"You could have spared yourself the trouble," replied the old lady.

"I often do," said FitzDuncan, "but I wanted to give you a last chance to win my gratitude."

"What makes it my last chance?" asked Agnes. "Are you about to burn the roof over our heads?"

FitzDuncan laughed and walked past them to study a tapestry that hung by the window.

"I know you have the second sight," he said, "so I have brought you a prophesy. You can tell me whether or not you believe it."

"Whose is it?" asked Agnes.

"Mine," said FitzDuncan, his eyes still on the tapestry. "I say that I will hold the feast of Yule this year in the castle of Egremont."

Agnes de Beauchamp sat with her mouth clamped shut.

FitzDuncan turned triumphantly. "You cannot deny it, can you?" he asked.

Agnes kept her silence.

"So you see," FitzDuncan continued, "I am lord of all Allerdale. The Runes must be mine, whether you like it or not."

"You are wasting your time," Agnes said impatiently. "I do not know what you mean, I do not know what you want, and I would not help you even if I did."

"I am a patient man," replied FitzDuncan. "I have waited years; I can wait another month. Besides, I must be over the sands to Galloway before the tide turns." He took a few steps towards the door, but paused and let his gaze linger on Adele. "So this is Adeline's love-child," he said. "How it must gladden your heart to have her with you."

"Stay away from my grand-daughter," snapped Agnes de Beauchamp.

"Oh, I bless her," FitzDuncan said merrily, and he was smiling as he left. The old lady looked indignantly at the sunlight pouring through the yellow skin of the window.

"Why Saint Kentigern does not send a tempest to drown him is beyond my understanding," she said.

"Why did he bless me?" asked Adele.

"He's no fool," said Agnes. "He knows what he owes to luck and the weakness of others."

"Is he a part of my story?" asked Adele.

"He is one of those who gained by it. I am the one who lost."

Adele met her grandmother's gaze and held it. "What did you lose?" she asked.

"Only my hopes," said Agnes. "In my day we had no choice in the matter of our husbands. We made the best of what we were given, and we played our part in the design until we were old enough to be the ones who made it for those who came after us. What your mother did was go against my design."

"She did not marry the man you chose for her?" asked Adele.

"No, she married him willingly enough," said Agnes bitterly. "She liked him for what he was, young and good-hearted – and he was bewitched by her. He worshipped the ground she walked on."

Adele closed her eyes. "What was his name?" she asked.

"Alan Waltheofsson. He stood to inherit Allerdale-below-Derwent. The lady of Egremont in those days was Cecile de Rumilly, my dearest friend, and all I wanted was to see our grandchildren grow up as neighbours. I wanted them to inherit the Cumbria we had spent our lives pulling from barbarism back into Christendom. Then the White Ship sank, and the world began to change. It brought King Henry on his one and only visit to Cumbria, and Walter Espec rode with him."

Agnes faltered, and impulsively Adele reached out her hands. The old lady smiled.

"I was merely wondering how to put it delicately," she said. "I do not know where your father first met Adeline. By the time a rumour reached me and I shook the truth out of her sister, it was too late. They were gone. If Adeline had fallen into my hands then I would have chained her to a wall until the madness passed, but instead I had the task of telling Alan Waltheofsson that his wife had fled."

Adele sank back in her chair and considered it all. "No wonder then that my parents never married," she said.

"Not even Thurstan would marry them after that," retorted her grandmother.

"What became of Alan Waltheofsson?" asked Adele.

The old lady gave a sigh and folded her hands in her lap. "He carried it well at first," she said, "but FitzDuncan paid an Irish harper to sing of it to Alan's face, and that broke him. FitzDuncan rules Alan's land as if it were his own, and when Alan dies childless, no doubt it will be."

Adele shivered. "Does my father know this?" she asked.

"He knows," said Agnes. "I was not in the least surprised when I heard he had taken to founding abbeys." She nodded grimly. "But the guilt is ours, not yours. We are the ones doomed to watch and suffer. The prayers of your father's monks will not save us, nor will they save Allerdale from William FitzDuncan."

"Is Maud de Rumilly in great danger?" asked Adele.

"You heard it from FitzDuncan's own lips. By Yule she will be a widow." Agnes de Beauchamp frowned and sat listening. "Does your knight know where to find you?" she asked.

"He will be here by nightfall."

"I think he may be here now," said Agnes. "I can hear a voice I do not recognise in the hall. Go and see who it is."

From her grandmother's chamber it was a dozen steps to the gallery of the hall. Adele ran to the banister and looked down to see Griselle caught up in the arms of a dark-haired young knight who was skirling her round the hall in a wild dance. It was only when the dance came to a halt that Griselle looked up and caught sight of her cousin, and when she called her name, the knight at her side gave a start and turned towards the gallery, the laughter draining from his face.

It was almost two years since Adele had last seen Robert de Brus.

8. PREACHING TO THE CHAINED

W e slowed our pace as we came in sight of Egremont. We wanted to study it from every angle.

"William Meschin knew how to build," Orm said approvingly. "There's no way in but the gate."

It was an impressive fortress, protected on three sides by a curl of the river, with a ditch to complete the ring of its defences.

"I wonder how many men Richard has left," said Orm.

"Last night I did not even count a dozen men-at-arms," I told him.

"Let's say he drags out the servants," said Orm. "That would make about twenty of them on the ramparts."

"Enough to hold the gate," I said, "but not for ever, and if twenty men were to climb the rampart somewhere else while the gate was under attack –"

"Look at the height of those walls," said Orm. "You'd need a long ladder, and we all know what happens to folk who try to climb into castles on long ladders. I reckon that if Richard had another sixty men, he could hold out a year."

"If he could only hold out until Easter," said Aimeric,

"it would be enough. Once the peace is law we could plead for him to King David – but David could not enter the quarrel now even if we took it to him; he would be accused of breaking his own truce."

"So all we have to do," I asked, "is find Richard of Egremont sixty men?"

The porter swung open the gate as we reached the bridge, and his shouts brought Ketel the steward into the bailey to greet us. He left us a moment in the deserted hall, then hurried back to lead us up to a chamber high in the keep-tower, where a fire was burning in an iron grate and where Richard and Maud rose to their feet and stared as if it were a hundred years since they had last set eyes on us.

"What is wrong?" asked Maud. "Why have you come back?"

"The prior told us your story," I replied.

"Then you were fools to listen," she said reproachfully.

"We had no choice," I said. "We already knew too much for our own peace."

"What did the good prior tell you?" asked Richard. "That I am doomed?"

"He told us of your quarrel with FitzDuncan," I answered. "He told us why your domain lies waste."

"Then why *have* you returned?" asked Richard. "I should have thought it would make you grateful to be riding away."

"It is not as easy as you might think," I said. "We hate FitzDuncan as much as you do."

"I doubt that," said Richard, and he looked at us with a sudden suspicion. "I suppose you have come to give me your advice?"

I nodded to Aimeric, and let him be the one to

expound our strategy. "The only counsel we can offer," he said, "is that you strive to endure until Easter. Once the peace is law, we will take your quarrel with FitzDuncan to King David. He will be your lord; he will have no choice but to give judgement on it, and his judgement will be fair."

"You forget one small thing," Richard said wearily. "King Stephen made me lord of Egremont and gave me the men to hold it. When war broke, I was already fighting FitzDuncan, and the war made that a fight with King David as well. David cannot in all honour let me remain. When he becomes lord of Cumbria by law, I will be the first of the dispossessed."

"Then why are you still here?" asked Aimeric.

"Because I would sooner die than leave Egremont to William FitzDuncan."

He gave a weight to every word. Aimeric was aghast. "That is madness," he protested.

I glanced at Maud, but she looked as if she were no longer listening. She was gazing into the shadows of the chamber where all manner of objects had been pushed against the walls to gather dust, among them a painted wooden cot and a rocking-horse with a jousting saddle and a harness with bells. I pictured her as a child – her brother Ranulf rocking her on the horse, the hall below bustling with William Meschin and his household – and I thought it no wonder she looked so haunted. Egremont for Maud must be a castle of ghosts.

"We were thinking," said Orm, "that with another sixty men, you could hold out a year."

Richard laughed. "I asked Thurstan for a hundred, but I would settle for sixty."

"Is there nowhere you could raise them?" asked Orm.

Richard shook his head. "There is no one left."

"How large is your domain?" I asked. "Surely you owe the service of several knights for it? Where are they all?"

Maud looked up. "My father held Egremont in return for the service of a single knight," she said. "His name was Godard de Boisville. He fought for us. His son is no more than a boy, still in wardship with a lord in the Vale of Eden."

"Arthur has returned," Richard told her. "He came home while you were on the road to Thurstan. Or so I hear," he added with a wry smile. "He has yet to come and swear me his oath of loyalty."

"He may not know what do to," said Maud. "He will be waiting for you to make him a sign."

"Well then, my lord," I said, "perhaps we should take him your summons?"

At daybreak we rode south, along the narrowing strip of land between the roots of the fells and the sea. Well after noon we came to the lip of a wide estuary. There was a village on the shore, and close by, ringed by a ditch and palisade, a huddle of timber buildings that only a harper out to flatter would call a castle.

"This must be Millom," said Orm. "The two of you should be enough to winkle out Arthur de Boisville. I'll see what I can learn in the village tavern."

The castle gate was open and unguarded. Aimeric and I rode in and tethered our horses by a water-trough in the bailey. A gust of greasy laughter came wafting out through the doorway of a porched and penticed hall, and as we walked towards it, a serving-woman came out with a tray of bowls. She took one look at Aimeric's cassock, spat on the ground and hurried by. He looked at me in bewilderment, but I was just as baffled.

We entered the hall and found seven men seated at the

high-table. Their dinner was long finished, but they had lingered to drink and their faces were flushed. Like a dog with seven heads they turned to stare at Aimeric's cassock, and the one who stared hardest was himself wearing the white woollen cassock of a monk.

"Messengers," he exclaimed with great hilarity. "The old cripple of York must be dead, and they are summoning me to the archbishopric."

From the chair beside him came a yapping noise. It was the tallest chair in the hall, and finely carved. Enthroned on it was a boy of about fourteen with lank red hair and a face infested with pustules. He looked at us, gave a belch, and thought this so amusing that he burst into another fit of yapping.

I waited until he had calmed, then I bowed with rather more respect than I felt he deserved. "Arthur de Boisville," I said, "I bring you the summons of your lord to attend him."

The boy looked uneasily at the monk, who contrived a hearty chuckle to reassure him and then addressed himself to us. "If you mean the coward who styles himself lord of Egremont," he said, "he is nothing but a usurper."

I kept my voice impassive. "Is that the message you wish us to take him," I asked Arthur de Boisville, "or would you care to come and say it to his face?"

"Are you proposing to take us by force?" the monk asked derisively, and it was then that I took in the other men at the table. The braiding of their hair and the colours of their clothes suggested that they were not from Cumbria, but from Galloway, and that could have only one meaning.

I glanced at Aimeric to see if he had drawn the same conclusion, but he was too angry to care. "What is your name?" he asked the monk.

"Wimund of Furness."

"You bring shame on your abbey."

"So my reverend abbot keeps telling me," retorted Wimund, to the merriment of his companions.

"It is not for the likes of you to call Richard of Egremont a coward," declared Aimeric. "He has endured three years of hell. You should be singing his deeds with pride."

"He has let better men die to save his own skin," said Wimund. "My lord Arthur's father rode to break the siege of Egremont and was cut down while Richard watched from the walls."

"Have you ever endured a siege?" I asked. "Do you know what it is to be penned helpless in your own stronghold?"

"Even if he is no coward," said the boy Arthur, "he is a usurper. I do not intend to die for him."

"It would certainly be going against the ways of nature," Aimeric told him. "The best thing for a worm like you would be to crawl under a stone and wallow in your own filth."

It was just the sort of insult to get us both killed, and it left me as dumb as those it struck. I had never seen Aimeric so filled with anger – he was always the one for taking the cruelty out of truth by musical irony and a smile – but now he began speaking in tongues.

"Ever since we crossed the Derwent," he told them, "we have seen nothing but the marks of evil. Every face we have looked into has been blighted by the hatred that plagues this land. On our road here we came to a hill where a castle stood in ruins, but it was the tidemark of war, and from that hill we at last saw land where nothing had been burned. I was moved to prayer. I thanked God that at least there was a corner of Allerdale that was free from evil." He raised a shaking hand and pointed at each of them in turn. "And now I come here and find it is peopled by wraiths. You are lost. You are letting evil eat away your souls. Unless you fight it now you are damned."

They sat through every word as if they had been speared to their seats. Arthur de Boisville writhed as if he could already feel the fires of hell. The one who fought back was Wimund the monk, but he had to gather his wits in a hurry to do it, and he was forced to drop his insolence.

"What brought you across the Derwent?" he asked. "Whom do you serve?"

"Archbishop Thurstan," replied Aimeric, "has sent us to be Maud de Rumilly's guardians."

The boy turned accusingly on Wimund. "You told me she had fled," he said. "You said she had run to her mother and that it was a sign they were broken –"

"How many are you?" Wimund asked us.

"Enough," said Aimeric. "So, are we to tell Thurstan that we find you among Maud de Rumilly's enemies?"

Wimund did not reply. The boy looked miserable and confused. Then I saw that they were staring over our shoulders, and a voice spoke behind us, from the doorway. "Answer them, Brother Wimund," it ordered.

Aimeric spun round; I forced myself to turn more slowly. The command had come from a man of Orm's age who was walking towards us, unfastening a golden disc-brooch encrusted with jewels that pinned his cloak. The warriors greeted him as if he were their leader, and as he folded his cloak over a chair one of them poured him a cup of ale. He had a haggard face and a leathery scar on his forehead; his eyes were pitiless, and it was hard not to flinch as he looked us up and down. This was clearly the man on whom the if and when of our leaving Millom unscathed would hang.

He refilled the cup and offered it to me. "You must be Simon de Falaise," he said.

I gave what I hoped was a dignified nod, took the cup and raised it in salute. "And yourself?"

"Cathal Duff," he answered. "My master warned me our paths might cross. He told me to remind you to go to him in Rath Sanas before you leave."

I gave another dignified nod, wondering how little I could get by with saying.

"These men serve Maud de Rumilly," blurted Arthur de Boisville.

Cathal Duff merely shrugged. "They can serve the queen of France for all I care. They have my master's safe-conduct to ride wherever they wish."

There was a clear message behind his words: that the power to grant safe-conduct through Allerdale-above-Derwent lay not with Richard of Egremont, but with FitzDuncan. Millom was now his. These men were here to hold it for him.

"Richard has summoned me," Arthur told his warder. "What am I to do?"

"Tell him you do not answer to a usurper," said Cathal Duff.

Arthur took a deep breath and faced us. "That is my reply to the usurper of Egremont," he declared.

"Then you are a fool as well as a knave," Aimeric told him. "Once FitzDuncan has devoured Egremont, you will be next."

"Not if I serve him well," said Arthur de Boisville, but he did not look as if he believed it. I felt a pang of pity for him. He was no more than a frightened boy trying to hold on to the domain that had been his father's in a ruthless world where the truth would rarely be what he wanted it to be. I wondered how long he would last.

Cathal Duff grinned. "Take Richard our greeting," he said. "Tell him it would need more than my good lord Arthur to save him."

I took hold of Aimeric and led him firmly towards the door. Cathal Duff's laughter rang in our ears.

In the village tavern we found Orm sharing a bench with two venerable Cumbrians he had evidently been plying with ale.

"Any luck?" he asked.

"We are lucky to be alive," I said. "I have a feeling we are going to find it hard to raise sixty men."

"Then we may as well be on our way," said Orm.

"Surely it is too late to reach Egremont before supper," said Aimeric plaintively, gazing at the pots on the hearthstone.

"Aye, but we'll only be riding half as far," said Orm, sweeping us outside with mysterious glee.

"Have you learnt something of the Runes of Alnerdal?" I asked.

"No one here has heard of them," he said, "but they've told me where to find a man who may."

9. THE RUNE-WEAVER

W e were more than halfway back to Egremont and the sun low over the sea when we turned inland – into a dale that must have been carved at the dawn of time by the slash of a giant's axe, with in the hollow of its trough a long and narrow lake as blue as sapphire and as deep as sorrow.

"They call it Wast Water," said Orm, "and here is its gatepost."

He drew rein at a tall stone that stood by the track. High on its face were carved three rows of letters. Aimeric peered at them and frowned.

"I cannot read this," he said. "Either it is too dark and I am too hungry or the letters make no sense."

"They are runes," said Orm. He ran his finger along them line by line. "They say, *Let any who ride on respect Freya*."

Aimeric made the sign of the cross, but the runes did not vanish. I peered at them myself, but was not surprised when I could make no sense of them. They were stark in shape, like bare trees or branches twisted together, chiselled into the rock and in-filled with paint.

We rode on along the lake-shore and a raven flew croaking over our heads. There was a track but no sign of any dwelling. On the far side of Wast Water there was not even a track; the lake lapped like a moat against sheer screes that fanned down from crags as tall as cathedrals.

"Look up there," I said. "If I were Richard of Egremont, that is where I would build my castle."

"It is a strange place to make sacred to the Earth Mother," said Aimeric. "In France her shrines are found where the land is gentle."

"I blame the pig-headed saints of the Church," said Orm. "Folk who follow the old ways are driven to the wilds."

Aimeric sighed. "So are many who follow new ways," he said. "It is not only the books of old wisdom that are burned."

We crossed a beck fringed with rowans, their leaves long gone but the berries hanging in shrivelled crimson clusters, and came to a lone farmstead with a rye-garth and a row of beehives. A girl ran inside as we approached, and a bald man with a brindled beard came to the door. He had only to stand on the threshold to block it, for he had a girth to match Orm's.

"Long life and luck to you," Orm greeted him. "Would you be Toki Freya's-Priest?"

"I'll not deny it," he said. "Who might you be?"

Orm told him our names. "We're asking a night's shelter," he said. "I'm told you're a wise man, and it may be that you can help us."

"These are troubled times," said Toki. "Food is scarce." He kept looking at Aimeric's tonsure and cassock. "And I've no liking for men of the Church," he admitted.

"Even when they are reeling in their saddles with hunger?" Aimeric asked him. "Orm read me the runes at the gate of the dale; I know this is Freya's place. I enter it humbly. I have not come to gather evidence to charge you with idolatry or heresy; I am a scholar, and I come in search of wisdom."

"Just answer me this," said Toki. "Who is the foremost of the gods?"

"He has many names," said Aimeric.

"How do they call him in Asgard?" asked Toki.

Aimeric swallowed unhappily, and my heart went out to him. I had grown up among the Norse folk of Cleveland and been weaned on tales of the old gods and heroes, but I could not answer Toki's question.

"Even in Asgard," said Aimeric, "the All-father has twelve names."

Toki was impressed, and Orm patted Aimeric on the shoulder. "This lad once spent fifteen weeks locked in a dungeon in Caerluel with my brother Hoskuld," he told Toki.

"I like a good tale," said Toki. "You can tell me over supper."

By the time we had stabled the horses it was dark but for a banner of golden light along the tops of the fells.

We settled ourselves on Toki's guest-bench and faced him across the hearth. His woman and two daughters sat beside him, watching us through the blue smoke of the peat-fire.

Toki raked the top off the fire to reveal a black cauldron buried in the glow. He hooked off the lid and the smell of kale-broth almost pinned me to the wall. I had only to close my eyes to be back in my home-village, for it was the smell of the winter nights of my childhood, the life I had lost when my father came to claim me. Toki took a leg of mutton from the rafters and cut long thin strips that he dropped into the stew; one of the girls pushed forward a bowl of dried mushrooms which he added by the handful; then he set the lid back on the cauldron, covered it again with sods, and we waited with watering eyes and watering mouths.

When we had eaten our fill, Toki brought out an elm-wood drinking-bowl with a silver rim and filled it with mead from a squat stone bottle. We drank in turn, and for a while spoke of everything under the sun but Allerdale. It was Toki, in the end, who brought us back as always to William FitzDuncan.

"Did you ride past Egremont?" he asked. "Have the Normans fled?"

"King Stephen's knights are gone," said Aimeric. "Richard remains."

"Not for long," said Toki. "FitzDuncan is letting it be known he will hold the feast of Yule in Egremont. I was hoping he might be there already."

"You sound as if you would welcome it," said Orm.

"I will," said Toki. "The sooner we are rid of our Norman lordling, the better. I have no time for Normans, apart from your good selves," he added, grinning at Aimeric and me.

"I am only half-Norman," I told him.

"And I am from Chartres," said Aimeric. "But tell me what makes FitzDuncan better in your eyes than a Norman. Myself I would prefer even a Norman to FitzDuncan."

"This is his land," said Toki. "He knows it. He feels it. He has the blood of its lords through his mother and through his wife. It is true that he is a harsh man, but these are times when a land needs a strong lord."

"If that is how you feel," said Orm, "you may be minded to help us. FitzDuncan has asked young Simon here to find him the Runes of Alnerdal."

Toki grinned. "What did I tell you?" he asked. "He

knows the land better than any Norman lordling ever will. Only a man with a good memory could set you such a fine test."

"You think he already knows the answer?" I asked.

"I'll say no more," said Toki, "except to say that your search will lead you back to him, for he is sitting on them."

"But what are they?" I asked.

"The Runes?" asked Toki. "They are a trail, a hidden path to hidden power."

"What do they say?"

Toki shrugged. "I do not know; I have never seen them."

"Then how do you know they lead to a hidden power?" asked Aimeric.

"I know who wrote them," said Toki.

"Who was it?" I asked.

Toki smiled and stroked his beard. "Does that tell you?" he asked.

For a moment I thought we were in for a game of riddles, but when none of us could answer him, Toki was crestfallen.

"Have you never heard tell of Ari Silkenbeard?" he asked.

"I have," said Orm. "He was a Viking of the great days. He used to keel his ships on Manannan. Some say he was a wizard."

"It is the truth," said Toki. "He found a power that changed him. Young, he was a killer, but when he came here he held the land in peace and ruled in wisdom. He lived to be old and died content."

"What was the power?" asked Aimeric. "Was it love?"

"No one knows," said Toki, "but it came from the Horn of Owain. That was the source of Ari's wizardry."

"The Horn of Owain?" I repeated.

"Ari wrote a song of his deeds," said Toki, "and in it there are these words:-

> "I cannot make you gifts
> of wave-tang or woman,
> I have no power over them;
> but come to me
> if you seek the Horn of Owain."

Aimeric grinned. "He speaks like a dragon curled up on its hoard."

"So he is," said Toki. "Before he died, Ari laid the Horn of Owain in a keeping-place and wrote the secret of the path to it in runes, so that only those with his wizardry would be able to follow it. That is the purpose of the Runes of Alnerdal – to lead whoever seeks it to the Horn of Owain."

Aimeric gripped my wrist. "I know where the trail must begin," he said. "Where Ari Silkenbeard lies buried."

Toki burst out laughing, but he was nodding in agreement.

"Why do you laugh?" Aimeric asked him.

"I can well believe FitzDuncan would give his heart to hold the Horn of Owain," he said, "but with all due respect, I cannot believe that he needs you to help him find the Runes."

"Why not?" asked Aimeric.

"Because he is sitting on them," said Toki. "Ari Silkenbeard was lord of Rath Sanas. He died in the very hall where FitzDuncan now sleeps."

That brought us to a halt, but Orm turned the talk to the lie of the fells, and he and Toki were soon drawing maps with charcoal on the back of a cutting-board. Aimeric caught my eye and glanced towards the door, and we slipped out as if to ease our bladders.

The sky was a tapestry of starlight, so bright that we could see the outline of the enclosing fells by the mass of their darkness. It showed us a path that led through oaks and rowans to the lake-shore, and we followed it, past rocks that moved and turned into sheep, until we came to the water's edge and stood marvelling. The lake had become a huge glittering mirror to the stars.

Aimeric turned to me exultantly. "We must find it," he said. "We must find the Horn of Owain and give it to him."

"To Richard?" I asked.

"No," he said. "To FitzDuncan."

"To make him twice as powerful?"

"To change him," said Aimeric. "Do you remember the words of the prior of Saint Bega? He said that the only way to save those in FitzDuncan's path is to save Fitz-Duncan from himself. Now we know how it can be done."

"By the Horn of Owain?" I asked. "What makes you believe in its power?"

"FitzDuncan believes in it," said Aimeric. "That is all that matters. He believes that Ari Silkenbeard was changed by the Horn of Owain – changed from a Viking killer into the ruler of a peaceful land –"

"You cannot change a wolf into a patriarch," I said dubiously.

"No one is beyond redemption," said Aimeric, "and why would he be searching for it unless he dreams of becoming like Ari Silkenbeard? If that is the dream of his innermost mind – to find wisdom and become the wise ruler of the land he loves – then we must do everything to help bring it about. That is how it must be, because the alternative is evil without end."

"You are sure that is how it would work?" I asked.

"If it works," said Aimeric, "it will be an act of sorcery." He looked nervously over his shoulder. "There are places in Christendom," he said, "where we would be burned at the stake for talking like this. It is as well we are on Freya's land."

"One thing is certain," I said. "Nothing short of sorcery will save Richard of Egremont."

A wolf howled at the head of the dale. We remembered where we were and hurried back to the farmhouse.

10. VICTIMS' GUILT

In the village of Gosforth there was a market of sorts, and the cooking-smells were too good to pass by. We bought a fresh loaf and a fried sausage and went to eat them in the churchyard, beneath a tall stone cross carved with warriors and serpents.

None of us were in a hurry to reach Egremont. I was wondering how to tell Richard that he was doomed.

He was waiting for us at a bridge on the road, with three mounted men-at-arms. He raised his hand in greeting, but before we could speak he spurred his horse along a track that ran upstream, and we followed like hounds on the heels of a stag.

Within a mile we came to a cluster of abbey buildings. They were deserted, silent, and bare. Sky gaped through smashed windows in walls blackened by burning, and it was in the remains of the cellarer's yard that Richard of Egremont dismounted to wait for us.

"I wish to speak with you alone," he told me; so I left Aimeric and Orm with the men-at-arms and followed him through a doorless arch into the shadows.

"This must be Calder Abbey," I remarked.

"Were you with Maud when she found the monks?"

asked Richard. "Are they prospering?"

"Not yet," I said, "but a friend of mine has promised them land."

The cloister was a desolate skeleton. Fallen slates snapped beneath our feet. Slimy rags of torn vellum manuscript flapped among the brambles that had overwhelmed the herb garden. Thurstan would have wept. Neither Richard nor I could find the courage to look the other in the eye.

"What did you find in Millom?" he asked.

"A frightened boy," I said, "and men from Rath Sanas to keep him in his place."

"So the southern gates are held against me?"

"FitzDuncan has you in a stranglehold," I said unhappily. "He is boasting that he will hold the feast of Yule in Egremont."

Richard took off his helmet and rubbed his nose with the back of his glove. With his grey hair hidden by his mail-coif, his face showed its youth in everything except a dry weariness around the eyes, like an apple beginning to wrinkle at the core.

"No one can stand alone against the tide," I said. "Cumbria is passing back to the Scots. It is not our doing, but nor is it ours for the unmaking."

"Then what is ours?" he asked.

"The choice," I said, "of whether we leap clear or whether we let the waves drag us under. No one will think less of you if you go to FitzDuncan and sue for peace."

"Is that what you advise?"

"It is the only counsel I can honestly give."

"It would be wasted," said Richard. "FitzDuncan will never grant me peace."

"If he would," I said, "would you go?"

Richard turned as if to beg me not to torment him, but then he frowned and looked at me searchingly. "When you took knighthood," he said, "did you make a vow?"

"Yes," I replied.

"In the words of Odilo de Cluny?"

"Yes."

"I made my vow to King Stephen," said Richard, gazing at his helmet and turning it in his hands. "It was in Westminster Hall, in the first days of his crowning. I was one of many, and if the truth be told, I had not won my place there by merit. Maud's mother asked it as a favour, and the same day I was given the domain of Egremont – but I made my vow, and a vow of my own to be true to it."

"And you have," I said, "through fire and storm."

Richard groaned. "Have I been a shield to widows and orphans?" he asked bitterly. "Have I been a shield to the Church when there is not an altar left in my domain that has not been robbed and fouled?"

"That is FitzDuncan's guilt, not yours," I argued. "You should see the lands he passed through in the war. Your doom is that Allerdale is where he comes home to roost. This is the quarrel to which he returns and returns."

"We share the guilt for it," said Richard, "and that is why the last drop of blood must be his or mine."

"The longer a battle lasts," I said, "the harder it becomes to retreat."

"There is no retreat when you are encircled," he retorted.

"When you are encircled," I said, "you cut your way out."

Richard shook his head. "By my reckoning," he said, "the only way to ensure they pay a price for my head is to force them to cut their way into Egremont to take it."

He said it wearily, without a trace of boastfulness. He was facing death with a courage that filled me with awe, but in the back of my mind I wondered if it were easier for him to face death than to break free and face life without honour. He seemed no longer even to be kicking against his fate. Either he had chosen his path, or it was a measure of how completely the years of fighting FitzDuncan had drained his will and crushed his spirit.

"I cannot stay and fight beside you," I said. "It would serve no purpose."

"Nor would I ask it," said Richard with a smile. "There is something far closer to my heart that I must ask of you. Take Maud away from here. Let her at least be spared the end." He pulled off his glove and drew a signet ring from his finger. "Take her this, and she will know you come from me. I will not return to Egremont until dusk, which will give you all the time you need to be away."

"Why will you not come with us?" I asked.

He avoided my beseeching eyes. "This is how it must be," he insisted. "Fare well, Simon de Falaise, and may you never be given a domain beyond your strength to hold."

"Come with us," I begged him.

"If you ever see me again," Richard said bleakly, "you will know that when it came to the end I screamed for mercy in the dirt at FitzDuncan's feet."

"No one will think less of you."

Richard shook his head. "Have you ever met Alan Waltheofsson?" he asked.

"I have heard the name."

"He is the true-born lord of Allerdale-below-Derwent. You would not believe it if you met him. When FitzDuncan breaks a man, he is broken for life."

* * *

Maud de Rumilly turned the ring in her fingers, then raised her eyes, showing me a face that was oddly serene.

"Do we leave at once?" she asked.

"Orm and Aimeric are waiting in the hall," I told her, for I had climbed alone to the chamber high in the keep. The fire had not yet been kindled, and the air was staled by the smell of damp tapestry.

Maud gathered a few belongings. "I will not need much," she said, "where I am going."

"Where will it be?" I asked.

"I have a choice," she said. "There are several fine nunneries in Yorkshire."

Gazing then into her face I realised I had grown to love her milky beauty and pale blue eyes. I could understand her wanting to turn her back on the world that had turned its back on Richard, but the thought of her locking herself in a nunnery made me ache with loss.

"That cannot be what Richard wants," I protested.

"Why should I do what he – " Maud began, only to stop herself and blush.

"When he will not do what *you* want?" I asked quietly. "Have you been begging him to leave?"

Maud found her saddle-bag and gripped it with a small white clenched fist. "It is more than that," she said. "I have my own guilt to purge. I brought this on Richard. If we had never loved it would never have happened."

"From what I hear," I said, "this was your mother's doing. She was the one determined to keep FitzDuncan out of Egremont. It was she who had Richard knighted and the barony bestowed on him."

"I should have spoken out louder and longer," said Maud. "I knew FitzDuncan well enough to know how it would end."

"Did Richard know?" I asked.

"He would not listen," said Maud. "He wanted to win me a domain, and once King Stephen had given him knights there was no turning back." She searched my face for the faintest sign of judgement. "I wanted him so much," she said, "and these were my mother's terms for letting me have him."

"Your mother has a lot to answer for," I said.

"Whatever she has done," said Maud, "she does not want it to end in Richard's death. She wants us to burn Egremont and flee."

"Then if your mother is telling him to leave," I said, "and you are telling him to leave – and King Stephen has abandoned him – why does he still refuse?"

Maud looked at me reproachfully. "What did you find in Millom?" she asked, and when I did not answer she nodded grimly. "Every road is watched. The only choice Richard has left is the manner in which he falls into FitzDuncan's hands. Let him at least choose the way of it."

"But surely if he were to ride out with us –"

"FitzDuncan hates him," said Maud. "Richard has held him at bay for so long. He has cost my brother-in-law dear in men and time and treasure. FitzDuncan will never let him leave." She looked at me with open misery. "I know what you must be thinking, Simon. I am the one who brought him to this; I should at least have the courage to stay with him to the end."

"This is not what he wants," I said, "and as you said yourself, we must let him choose the way of it." I took a step towards the door, but she made no move to follow. "If I were Richard," I said, "I would only need to look at you to know how much I wanted to live."

Maud gave me the saddest of smiles. "Even if I could

pull him free," she said, "I can never have what I want."

"What is that? Egremont?"

"What do you take me for?" she asked. "No. I lost Egremont the day my brother died. All I want with Richard is what any woman wants with the man she loves, and it can never be while there is hatred between Richard and FitzDuncan."

"Why not?"

"Would you have this last for ever?" asked Maud. "A boy born to us would grow up hating his cousin – for Alice has given FitzDuncan a son – and the curse would flower again as soon as they reached manhood. My father's grandchildren would grow up sworn enemies."

That silenced me. When I understood, I knew she was right. It was better that the quarrel end, whatever the price.

"It is only women who see so far," I said. "Men are blinded –"

"Listen!" she interrupted me, and I heard the sound of someone running up the stairs. I reached the door and flung it open, causing Aimeric – who had paused to knock – to step backwards in surprise. I had to grab a fistful of his cassock to stop him tumbling down the stairs.

"There is a herald at the gate," he told me, "and he is asking for you by name."

I glanced at Maud, but she had resumed the cool and distant look I now knew was no more than a mask to stop her despair from showing in her eyes.

"Follow me," she said. "I will take you the quickest way."

She led us to a door that gave straight onto the walkway of the ramparts. We had only to follow the curving palisade to reach the penticed embrasures above the gate, where Orm and Ketel the steward were waiting in the shadows.

I looked out to see one of FitzDuncan's warriors at the far end of the bridge, a peeled hazel-wand in his sword-hand as the sign that he came in peace.

"I am Simon de Falaise," I called. "What do you want of me?"

"My master summons you to Rath Sanas," he answered. "He bids you sup with him tonight in his hall."

"Tell him to go to hell," whispered Maud.

"We cannot afford to refuse," said Orm, and he gave me a look charged with meaning. I turned to Aimeric, who gave a faint grin followed by a shiver.

"Wait there," I called down to the herald. "We will ride out when we are ready."

Maud laid her hand on mine. "What are you to my brother-in-law?" she asked.

"It looks as if we are about to find out," I said. "You must trust us not to lose our souls."

"FitzDuncan will try to make you drop your guard," she warned me. "However much you find yourself saying, do not let him see into your heart."

We had left our horses saddled in the bailey, so we had only to mount and ride out. The herald led us along the northern road, and at the first fringe of woodland we came to he gave a shrill whistle. Out of the trees and onto our heels rode five warriors with hunting-bows and full quivers. Their leader raised the palm of his hand to us in greeting, and they fell into a pace that matched our own, riding behind at a respectful distance, like an armed escort for honoured guests.

11. THE SECRETS OF RATH SANAS

Night had fallen by the time we reached Rath Sanas, but the moonlight through a thinning cloud showed me the hog's bristle of ramparts as we rode up to the gates.

In the bustle of the stables, Orm brushed against me and muttered into my ear. "In the hall, let's go separate ways. I'll sit at one of the lower tables with my feet on our bags."

We washed and joined the throng of folk who were making their way towards the upper end of the bailey, where a bodhran-beat and bray of pipes came from the torchlit doorway of the hall. I did not even try to count the number of fighting-men. Most of them were young and lean and swaggering, rootless men from the hills of Galloway who would serve any master who promised them reward. We had killed them by the thousand in the Battle of the Standard, but there would always be more. There were a few older men, finely-dressed, their ladies encrusted with gold and jewels, the plunder of the war.

The hall was timbered and ancient, high-roofed with smoke-blackened beams and carved pillars. It was crowded with tables, but Aimeric and I followed the herald towards the one set apart on a dais at the northern end. There we waited until the music stopped, a curtain was pulled back from an inner doorway, and the lord and lady of Rath Sanas entered hand in hand.

Alice de Rumilly took my breath away. She was taller than Maud; her hair was burnished gold and her eyes a midsummer green. What struck me most was her pride. She carried herself like a woman who had all she desired – and William FitzDuncan looked every bit as proud as he walked at her side.

"Why is there no justice in this world?" whispered Aimeric.

FitzDuncan greeted us gaily, and named us to the lady Alice. "We must be gentle with them," he told her. "They visited me once in Caerluel, and I had them thrown into the cellars before the meal was even served. It is bold of them to return to my table."

They took their places in two high-backed chairs, and Alice made a sign for me to sit facing her. The moment we were seated, the music resumed and the servers hurried forward. I looked for Aimeric and saw him several trenchers away, sitting with the chaplain – for FitzDuncan even had a chaplain, a wrinkled man as bald as an egg, whose hair I assumed had fallen out when FitzDuncan confessed his sins.

The meal opened with a dish of spiced trout. We were served with wine from a swan-necked silver flagon. I was tempted to propose a toast to the folk huddled in bothies by Saint Bega's Priory. Instead I ate, staring at my food, my cheeks burning with embarrassment.

When I gathered my courage and raised my eyes, I found Alice waiting to catch my gaze. "How is my sister?" she asked.

"Suffering," I said.

"Well she may," said Alice, in an untroubled voice that set my teeth on edge. She saw me struggling to master the look on my face. "Tell me what Mother and Maud have told you," she suggested, "and I will tell you what is true."

"I have never met your mother," I replied, "and the rights and wrongs of her designs for Allerdale are nothing to me. I speak from what I have seen. I have witnessed nothing but suffering since I came to Allerdale."

"Maud has only herself to blame," said Alice. "She should never have let herself be used against us."

She spoke dismissively, without guilt or mercy, and I was too disgusted to reply.

FitzDuncan had been listening, and he chose the moment to join in, speaking for all the world like a genial host who could not bear unpleasantness at his table. "Did I not warn you, Simon, that this is a family quarrel?" he asked. "Be thankful it does not run in your blood."

I tried to match his lighter tone; it seemed the safest course. "I have never been more thankful," I said, "to be no more than a stranger passing through."

Everyone laughed, and the moment passed. A dish of spit-roast boar was set on the table, and FitzDuncan cut it deftly into steaming succulent slices.

At the end of the meal, after pastries that left us licking our fingers, Alice bid us goodnight and rose to retire. By the hearth, a harper began to play, and Aimeric turned in his seat to listen.

FitzDuncan refilled my cup. "Where will you be feasting Yule?" he asked.

"In Elmeslac," I replied. "Do you know it?"

"I know Walter Espec. Do you serve him?"

"He and Archbishop Thurstan are my lords."

FitzDuncan affected great interest, and I wondered if

even this were saying too much. My mouth clamped shut, and the conversation withered.

"I can see we are wasting our time with small talk," said FitzDuncan. "Tell me what you have learnt of the Runes of Alnerdal?"

I did my best to savour my chance to intrigue him. "This is a fine hall," I said, admiring the rafters. "I hear it was built by a man named Ari Silkenbeard."

FitzDuncan grinned. "Some say he was a wizard."

"And that his greatest treasure was the Horn of Owain," I added. "It is a good tale, but myself I would set no store by it unless I knew who Owain was, and if he ever lived."

"Oh, he lived," said FitzDuncan. He made a sign to the harper, who broke with his tune by running his fingers across the strings. "Sing us the Sister's Lament," Fitz-Duncan told him.

The harper was pot-bellied and snaggle-haired, with a nose like a parsnip, but his fingers were long and quick. He plucked notes that rose like stairways of birds, and he sang to their rise, making his words arc like arrows in flight.

> *"Owain is gone.*
> *He was the eagle.*
> *He was my brother, and he was brave.*
> *Owain, it is autumn.*
> *Red-brown the bracken, yellow the stubble.*
> *I have lost that which I love.*
> *Strong is the wind.*
> *Cold are the hearth-stones.*
> *I will weep, and then be silent."*

The harper's fingers skirled, then the notes came fewer and fewer, like the last tears of eyes weeping themselves dry.

Aimeric sat transfixed and transfigured, as if he had seen the angels of heaven. A moment later he had crossed the floor and was sitting like a disciple at the harper's feet.

"There are other songs," FitzDuncan told me. "Owain was king of Cumbria. He won a hundred battles, but he died fighting the English. It was long ago, but he will never be forgotten. Dunmail, the last king of Cumbria lived in Ari Silkenbeard's day, and Ari fought beside him. When their last battle was lost, Dunmail forsook his kingship and entered a monastery. He gave his sword to his foster-brother, who threw it into a tarn on the heights of the fells, and the Horn of Owain he gave to Ari."

"What makes you seek it?" I asked.

"Have you never heard," asked FitzDuncan, "of the chalice that gives whoever drinks from it eternity in life and life in eternity? Such is the Horn of Owain. I have wanted it ever since my uncle Waltheof told me the tale when I was a boy. Two dreams have woven the web of my life: to find the Horn of Owain, and to be king of the Scots."

"I for one, my lord, pray that you are never king of the Scots."

"So, to my regret, do many others," said FitzDuncan with a grin, "and they fear me because of the truth to my claim. My father was king, and his murder went unavenged – but if I cannot have power, then let me find wisdom instead. Let me have the Horn of Owain."

"For any other, I would offer to find it," I said, "but not for a man about to break the kings' truce by striking the last blow against Egremont."

"This quarrel is older than the war," FitzDuncan said impatiently. "I do not consider it bound by the truce. Once it is settled, I will keep my uncle David's peace as lord of Allerdale, taking to my weapons only when he calls me – and he will call me. He needs me enough to let me settle my quarrels, just as your masters need peace so badly that they will do nothing to save the lordling usurper of Egremont."

"Let him go in peace," I said, "and I will find you the Horn of Owain."

FitzDuncan sat forward. "So you believe it can be found?"

"I believe in my companions," I said. "Aimeric has read every book ever written, and with me also is a rune-master named Orm. Let Richard go in peace, and we will stay until we have read every rune-stone in Cumbria."

"I think you over-value your services," FitzDuncan warned me.

I contrived a shrug. "That is for you to decide, my lord," I said as if I hardly cared, "but I would do it for no less. Since Aimeric and Orm are with me, I judge it worth making the offer, but I would far rather be riding home. As you said yourself, this is a family quarrel."

FitzDuncan levelled a finger at me. "Find me the Horn of Owain, *then* you may haggle over Richard. Who knows what it may change?"

It had the ring of a bargain struck before witnesses. I felt the weight of commitment and had to struggle to keep my confidence. "I would be interested," I said, "to see where Ari Silkenbeard lies buried."

FitzDuncan rose to his feet and snapped his fingers. "Nechtan, Cormac, light torches and come with us."

I beckoned to Orm, who came lumbering up the hall, but it was no easy matter to reach Aimeric. He was lost in all the harper was telling him. We tore him away and followed FitzDuncan out into the bailey. A light rain was falling, and the torches hissed as they burned.

We entered a steep-roofed little chapel, where the

torches burned with tall straight flames, illuminating carved and painted walls and an altar-cloth in purple and gold from which the faces of saints stared with dark round eyes.

"Ari spent his youth plundering churches," said FitzDuncan, "and his last years building one." He held out a hand to stop us walking further and pointed at the floor. "See for yourselves how he marked his grave."

Even though the chapel was of timber, the floor was paved, and set among the flags was a grave-slab of green slate the length of a man. Chiselled on its surface was a wheel-headed cross whose outline was a pattern of plaited serpents. I could see no mark on it anywhere that even faintly resembled a rune.

"Do you wish to say a prayer," asked FitzDuncan, "or shall we return to the hall?"

"Seeing takes longer than looking," said Orm. "Is there a candle or a lamp to hand?"

A candle was found in a niche in the wall, and when it was alight Orm stood it at the hub of the wheel-head of the cross. He got down on all fours and snuffled at the slab, studying it from every side.

He gave a grunt of satisfaction. "Here they are," he said, "a whole string of them."

Aimeric and I dropped down beside him and stared. I would never have found them myself, for they were no more than a place where the even notchings of a serpent's scales grew branches and became runes.

"Can you read them?" asked Aimeric.

Orm worked his fingers slowly along their length, muttering into his beard. "I can read them," he announced. "They say, *If you love this land, drink to it from the Horn of Owain. All I ask for fame is that you take it from my hands.*"

Aimeric shuffled backwards and looked at the slab in

horror. "That can have only one meaning," he said. "The Horn of Owain is in there with him."

Orm was already running his fingers along the slab's edge. "There are the marks here of a wrench," he said. "It looks as if we are not the first to read the runes."

"Well done," said FitzDuncan. "You have come as far as I have travelled myself. I had the grave opened, but I found nothing but the weapons and bones of a warrior."

"Nothing at all?" asked Aimeric.

"There were signs," said FitzDuncan. "Ari sleeps on his back, but his hands rest on his hips and his fingers are spread. Beneath them, his tunic is creased as if a casket had rested on his lap. Someone must have opened the grave and taken it gently – and it was all they wanted, or they would have taken Ari's ring." He held out his hand and we saw the ring on it, a head of the Virgin carved on a green jewel and set in gold.

"I once bought one like that," said Orm. "I gave it to a woman in Calabria in exchange for her horse. I've often wondered what her husband said when she got home."

"How large is the casket?" asked Aimeric.

"Too small to hold the Horn itself," said FitzDuncan, "but a casket from Ari's hands will be carved – richly carved – and there will be runes in its designs." He looked at me keenly. "Find me the man who came here before us. If he is dead, bring him to me alive. Even if you cannot find him, bring him to me."

"How long do we have?" I asked.

"Three days," said FitzDuncan.

"But that is no time at all," protested Aimeric.

"Is a man of the Church telling me that miracles cannot be worked in three days?" FitzDuncan asked him. "Three days, or as long as you wish, according to whether or not you want the fate of the usurper of Egremont to be part of our bargain."

We returned somewhat silently to the hall, where FitzDuncan instructed his steward to find us a lodging, then he bid us goodnight.

As we were shouldering our saddle-bags, a girl came up behind me and tugged at my sleeve. I turned with incredulous hope, but I was mistaken.

"The lady Alice asks that you attend her at daybreak," she said. "You will find her in the chapel."

I bowed and the girl made to leave. "Wait," I begged her. "I am searching for a friend named Catriona. Have you any word of her?"

She looked puzzled. "I have served here a year, my lord, and I have never even heard the name."

I thanked her and followed the others to a hostel where we sprawled on covered straw pallets and talked until our eyes began to close but we were no nearer to the Runes of Alnerdal.

"I heard what you asked that lass," Orm told me. "You'll not find Catriona here. She has the wits never to return."

"For a moment I thought it was her," I said. "That is how she haunts me. I keep seeing her shadow."

"What haunts you," said Aimeric, "is the ghost of your love. It is high time we took you back to Adele."

"Sablegarde," I said with a groan. "I told Adele we would be with her by sunset."

"Tonight?" asked Aimeric.

"The day before yesterday," I said miserably.

"Never mind," said Orm. "The longer you make them wait, the happier they are to see you."

I lay back and conjured visions of Adele, and a

memory came from the days of my wound-fever in Elmeslac after the Battle of the Standard: Adele as she had been then, holding back the tresses of her hair as she bent to kiss my forehead before she left with the lamp. She was my healer, my guardian angel, and I called on her under my breath, begging her to protect me from the demons of Rath Sanas.

12. THE WAYS TO WOUND

R ain was spouting off the eaves when I opened the door of our hostel. I cupped my hands and caught enough to wash my face, then pulled my cloak over my head and made a run through the mud for the chapel.

The chaplain was kneeling before the altar reciting sacred words of Latin in the echoing accent of the folk of the Irish Sea. I knelt by the door, behind three women who were the only others there. The rain had soaked the shoulders of their cloaks and given the linen cloths they wore filleted on their heads the transparence of veils. I knew Alice by the long golden plait in which her hair was bound, and beside her knelt the girl who had brought me her summons.

While they prayed I looked at the carved and painted panels on the wall. For a moment I thought they told a Viking saga, but it was only because Christ fishing on the Sea of Galilee bore a strong likeness to a carving I had admired in the hall the night before depicting Thor fishing for the Midgard Serpent.

The chaplain rose and gave us his blessing, laying his hand on each of our heads in turn. When he left, two of the women followed, leaving me alone with Alice de Rumilly.

"I was harsh with you last night," she said. "Please forgive me."

"It was I who was discourteous," I replied.

"You made me feel my guilt," Alice confessed. "I cannot deny my part in this, but there are things I would have you know. You will ride away and tell the world what you have seen in Allerdale. I know how William will be judged, and that is why I must speak for him now, for he will never defend himself."

I was speechless. It appeared she was about to give me a list of FitzDuncan's virtues.

"William is his own enemy," she said. "He is at war with himself. He is haunted by his father yet ashamed of him, and he believes his own life must be the revenge as well as the healing for all his father suffered. I thought when we met that I could heal him, but I know that it is a curse with a hold on all his family."

"Something of the kind haunts his uncle David," I agreed.

"With William the scars are deep," said Alice. "His father was king of the Scots, but only because he rode north with Norman knights to back his claim. William is haunted by the shame of his death. The Scots called him a usurper, and he paid a usurper's price."

"Is that why FitzDuncan hates all Normans?" I asked. "Because we let his father ride to his death?"

"It is why he strives so hard to be a Scot," said Alice, with what was almost a glint of bitterness. "It is why he must hunt with the hardest and kill with the cruellest, because he is driven to prove to them that he belongs – but that is not why he hates us. He hates us because we have the power to demand that the rest of the world be like us. When we do, William is bound by his nature to rebel."

"We all have our hauntings," I said, "but we are judged by our deeds."

"All I ask you to understand," Alice said with sorrow, "is why on the day Egremont falls, William will give way to the howling of his men. He will act by their custom. He will make Richard pay the usurper's price, even though he knows the barbarism of it."

It was only then that I understood. "What is the usurper's price?" I asked. "What did the Scots do to FitzDuncan's father?"

Alice looked at me with all the horror of a woman knowing that the same could one day happen to her husband or son. "They blinded his eyes and cut off his hands," she said. "He died within days."

Neither Aimeric nor Orm were in the hostel. I ran to the hall, stopping in the doorway to shake my cloak. FitzDuncan was sitting on a bench talking urgently with a knot of his warriors. He stopped as soon as he saw me.

"I thought you would be gone by now," he greeted me. "Do not wait for the rain to stop. It can last a week."

"I seem to have lost my companions," I said.

"Your scholar-friend went off with my harper," said FitzDuncan. "I have not seen your rune-master."

I reached for a stool and sat down facing him, with the ashes of the hearth between us. I could tell my presence was keeping them from their talk.

"Have I still your safe-conduct to ride wherever I wish in Allerdale?" I asked.

"I give you three days," said FitzDuncan.

I hated him then. I hated him for his power and his luck and his twisted purpose, and it showed in my face. FitzDuncan smiled to himself.

"Ride wherever you wish," he said pleasantly. "I know I can trust you not to leave Cumbria before the wedding of your friend."

"Which friend is that?" I asked.

"Robert de Brus. Is he not a friend of yours?"

I grinned with surprise and delight. "So Robert has come to take up his domain of Annandale?" I asked.

"Yesterday he was in Caerluel," replied FitzDuncan, "making known his betrothal to a girl he met at Sablegarde."

"Is that so?" I asked, fighting to keep the grin on my face. "It is good to know there is still joy in the world."

I walked out into the rain and hurried to the hostel. Orm and Aimeric had still not returned, but I was glad of it: I slumped onto the bed and buried my face in the pallet.

The longer I thought, the more convinced I became that FitzDuncan knew the meaning for me of every word he had just said.

I could see it all in my mind's eye: the look on Robert's face as he found her, and the look on Adele's when she saw how he had changed. It was a year and more since they had seen each other, and Robert was no longer the awkward youth whose longing for Adele had grown so tortured that it broke their friendship. The war had changed Robert more than any of us, but I knew all that would have been rekindled for him by their meeting.

I reached for Aimeric's shoulder-bag and searched it for something to write with. The first thing that came to hand was a stick of chalk. Aimeric had taught me my letters, even if I would never know how to spell half the words I spoke. On a plank of wall above the bed I wrote *Simon*, then drew an arrow and wrote *Adele*. It was the first time I had ever written her name.

Then I took my saddle-bag and ran to the stables.

I found her in the hall of the castle of Sablegarde, which I reached after a drenching gallop through Allerdale-below-Derwent, asking the way from the few folk I met on the quagmire roads.

Her hair was wet, newly brushed and hanging loose, and she was frowning in concentration as she hung sodden cloaks to dry over a length of twine that had been strung between two pillars. The wide-cut sleeves of her gown had slipped back to her elbows, and I could see the three silver bracelets on her wrist. One of the cloaks she had hung had an embroidered hem I recognised: it was the very same that Robert de Brus had been wearing the last time I saw him.

Adele gasped when she saw me. No one in the hall was paying us any mind – there were children playing a noisy game of draughts at one of the tables, and women moving to and fro – but she did not run towards me, nor did she give the faintest sign of joy. She was staring at the look on my face, and she tensed as if she were afraid of me. I stopped six paces from her, for I suddenly felt I had no right to go closer.

"What is wrong?" she asked. "Where are Aimeric and Orm?"

"They are following," I said. "Many things are wrong. How have the days gone with you?"

"Well," she said, with a relieved smile. "They have been rich."

"All you hoped?"

"Yes."

"You kept your design well hidden," I said. "I never guessed."

Adele's eyebrows went down like a helmet rim. "What have I ever hidden from you?" she asked.

"I can only wonder," I said. "The night you came to me in York and told me the tale of your long-lost grandmother, you did not tell me she lived a mere crossing of the sands away from Robert de Brus."

"How dare you?" Adele asked incredulously. "Do you think we are all like you?"

"What do you mean by that?" I asked.

"You said you would return by nightfall on the second day," she said, with anger boiling into her voice. "Three nights have gone by since. How many of them have you spent in Rath Sanas?"

"One," I said, "but what is that to you? What do you know of Rath Sanas?"

"I know it is the castle of William FitzDuncan," said Adele, "and I know the search that took you there."

"How?" I asked. "Who told you?"

"So you would not have told me yourself?"

"Who told you?" I repeated.

"Robert," said Adele.

"How does he know?" I asked.

"He was there," Adele said furiously.

"Where?" I asked in bewilderment.

"In Caerluel," she said, "the day you asked Fitz-Duncan – before half the knights of the Scottish royal court – if he would give you one of his serving-girls. Robert watched you ride out with her perched on the cantle of your saddle."

"That was a year ago," I protested. "I did not go to Rath Sanas to find Catriona."

"No?" asked Adele. "When you were there, did you make no search for her?"

I looked imploringly at her, begging her to stop.

"Robert told me," she said, "that he quarrelled with you because he opened the secrets of his heart to you and you gave nothing in return. I can understand his bitterness."

As if she had summoned him, I heard Robert calling my name. He was walking towards me across the hall, and beside him, her hand in the crook of his arm, her gown whisking the rushes and on her face a look of utter happiness, walked Adele's cousin Griselle.

I saw then what FitzDuncan had done, and turned with a groan to Adele. "This is all a mistake," I said.

"Yes," she said angrily. "I thought I understood you, and I thought you understood me. Clearly I was mistaken."

She walked away, smiling at Robert and Griselle as she passed them, making for the doorway from which they had come. From outside came the sound of horses in the bailey. Robert had clapped me on the shoulder and was halfway through his greeting before the look on my face brought him to a halt.

"What is wrong?" he asked.

"He knew," I said, as much to myself as in reply. "He must have read my mind in the night and found the way to break me."

"I'll break you," came Orm's voice behind me, and I turned to see him entering with Aimeric, Arnoul, and Hemming. Orm reached out, gripped me by the surcoat and pulled me towards him so hard I almost bit the tip off my tongue. "Never do that to me again," he warned me.

I felt shamed in front of all my companions. It even hurt to face Aimeric's compassionately questioning eyes.

Orm saw it, and let go of me. "Anyhow," he said, smoothing my surcoat, "we're well out of Rath Sanas. A fresh bunch from Galloway rode in as we rode out. FitzDuncan now has the men to take Egremont apart timber by timber."

PART THREE
The Land of Lost Names

13. ORM'S PATH

R obert de Brus took me by the arm and led me out of the castle, and his mood changed the moment we were alone. He walked ahead in silence, along a track through the marshes that came to an end at a fish-garth where two men were wading with a net. Beyond the dunes, the Solway was bare mud, veined like a leaf with dark channels of water. The rain had stopped, but the low clouds were thickening the dusk.

"You have only yourself to blame," Robert said sharply.

"For what?" I asked, for there seemed so many things.

"For getting yourself wounded by FitzDuncan," said Robert. "For God's sake, Simon! Last year he had you tossed into his dungeon. Surely that was enough to teach you how to treat him? Here in Cumbria he is a power unto himself. No one goes against him."

"Richard of Egremont goes against him," I retorted.

Robert gripped me by the shoulder. "Listen to me," he said. "If you stand beside Richard, you will be buried with him. I cannot help you."

"I was not asking you," I said roughly. "You could have helped me in other ways, by sparing Adele the tale of how I rode out of Caerluel with Catriona on the cantle of my saddle."

Robert laughed. "I knew it," he said. "She has you dancing like a bear. I fell for it once. I loved the way she drifted through the days like a sleeping princess waiting for a saint in shining armour to come and kiss her awake. I tried to be the saint and it almost killed me. If you want to make the same mistake, by all means waste your life trying, but I told her about Catriona to show her you are flesh and blood like the rest of us."

"Thank you," I said. "I wish you were head-down in that fish-garth."

"You can do better than Adele," said Robert. "Find yourself a woman who will love you for what you are."

"Is that what you have found in Griselle?" I asked.

"Yes," he said, "and I cannot tell you how good it is."

"It must have been a very sudden illumination," I said. "You did not speak of her when we met a month ago in Rocksburgh."

"You are the one who taught me to hide the secrets of the heart," said Robert with a smile. "I met Griselle at the summer's end. Since I was made lord of Annandale, half the nobles of Scotland have been setting their daughters beside me at table."

"So your families approve?" I asked.

"Now we have told them, they are acting as if they are the ones who brought it about. We are to be married in splendour by Bishop Aethelwold himself."

"Tell me about Annandale," I said. "What is it like, your domain?"

"If it were not so dark," said Robert, pointing across the Solway, "you could see it from here. Much of it is forest: you can ride it from end to end without once leaving the shade of the trees. There are elk-deer and brown bear, and the men of Galloway for neighbours." He stared into the dark distance. "That is why I cannot help you. I know that no man deserves the end Richard of Egremont is facing, but FitzDuncan draws his men from Galloway, and if I rode against him with mine, I would be broaching blood-feuds that would follow me home to my own lands."

"I know," I said, "and that is the last thing in the world I would wish you as a wedding-gift – but is there no one in Cumbria who has feuded with FitzDuncan and is longing for the chance to strike him?"

Robert shook his head. "All those who have feuded with FitzDuncan are broken men."

"Why does King David do nothing to stop him?"

"According to Hugh de Morville," said Robert, "David believes that the sooner FitzDuncan has Egremont, the sooner his war-band will shrivel and go home, and the better it will be for Cumbria."

"I'll pray he's right," I muttered, "for all our sakes."

Robert put his arms across my shoulders and we turned back towards the castle. "One thing is certain," he said. "You and I must never again be enemies."

Over supper I came face to face with Agnes de Beauchamp. She was presiding over the meal in place of the lord and lady of Sablegarde, who were in Caerluel, and she questioned me intently about Richard and Maud.

"Do you happen to know what Cecile de Rumilly has told them to do?" she asked.

"Flee," I said.

"It would be wise," the old lady agreed. "Your task," she said, "must be to take them south by way of Furness, and

I would advise you not to stop until you are safe in Cecile's castle of Skipton."

"It cannot be done," I said. "FitzDuncan has men at Millom."

"It could be done with Maud," added Aimeric, "but not with Richard."

"Then Richard's only hope is to disguise himself as a woman and take a coracle to Ireland," said Agnes de Beauchamp. "You will never bring him out past Rath Sanas."

"Is there no other road out of Allerdale?" I asked.

"None," she said.

"I know a road," announced Orm. "There are high scarths with cairned tracks leading over the fells to Borrowdale, and once you're down Borrowdale you're not far from the Vale of Eden."

"But the fells are a wilderness," protested Aimeric. "We could be caught in the head of those dales like deer in a park."

"While you were singing to the moon by Wast Water," Orm told him, "I was talking over the lie of the land with Toki the priest. What he told me and what I know myself fit together. I can guide you through the fells, and there's even a chance I know them better than FitzDuncan."

"Then there's our road," I said triumphantly.

"Richard must be saved," said Agnes de Beauchamp, "and FitzDuncan robbed of his revenge. That is all that matters." Her eyes were sparkling as if she were tempted to ride with us. "Between Borrowdale and the Vale of Eden," she said, "lives a man named Forne Ligulfsson. He will not ride out against FitzDuncan to save a Norman, but he will grant you protection the moment you set foot on his land."

"I know him," said Orm. "Forne of Greystoke. He will trade us fresh horses."

I sat back in a flush of determination, my pulse racing at the vision as it came clear. I believed we could do it, and it was all I wanted now; to save Richard and to lose myself in the task, to be consumed by a purpose that would leave me no time to think of anything else.

Before I knew it, I found myself looking at Adele. I had been avoiding her eyes all through supper, and she had avoided mine, for she had taken care to sit well away from me. Now I caught her staring at me, her eyes dark and full of foreboding.

"Do you still wish to return with us to Yorkshire?" I asked her, and as I spoke I understood the rules of courtesy. They must have been invented to help people step neatly over open wounds.

Adele nodded, but the answer was in her silent face. She looked as if she were longing for home.

"Then you must travel to Greystoke by a safer road," I told her. "Aimeric will go with you, and you must wait for us there."

"Why me?" protested Aimeric.

"Because your head is full of learning," I told him, "and too precious to risk – and if we vanish, it will be your task to go to Bishop Aethelwold and raise the hue and cry."

"It may seem strange," said Aimeric, "but I only feel safe when I am with you."

"You will have Arnoul and Hemming," I said.

Orm was nodding in agreement. "The fewer we are in the fells, the better," he said.

"I'll not go with them," declared Adele. "I will come with you."

My tongue tied with surprise and my longings went to

war with my wits. "No," I said wretchedly, "it is out of the question."

"Why?" asked Adele, and I knew by the look she gave me then that she was determined to win if I made it a contest of wills. "I can ride as fast and as far as you," she said defiantly.

It was true; she was stronger than Aimeric. "Why do you wish to come?" I countered.

"To be with Maud," she said, but she smiled when my face fell. "And with you," she added with a sniff of reluctance. "The manner in which you came back to me today proves that I cannot let you safely out of my sight."

That silenced me. I turned to Orm, but he only grinned. "I say women are lucky," was his judgement.

"The fell-folk will be less wary of you if there are women among you," agreed Agnes de Beauchamp. "I will pray for your success." She rose to her feet and held out her hand to Adele. "We must have one last hour," she said, and they left the hall together.

When the tables had been cleared, I sat with Aimeric by the fire while Orm told Arnoul and Hemming the lie of the land and the roads to Greystoke. Aimeric brought out his lute and began plucking mournful skeins of notes.

"You sound like FitzDuncan's harper," I told him.

"He offered to take me as his pupil," said Aimeric. "He said he would teach me everything he knew."

"Were you tempted?" I asked.

Aimeric laughed. "He also said it would take thirteen years. An Irish harper's craft is deep, all of it unwritten and taught by word of mouth from one to another. Among what they learn is a body of lore they call the Dinshenchas, so vast that no one harper can ever know it all. It tells how every place in Ireland came by its name."

"Is there a Dinshenchas for Cumbria?" I asked.

"That is the very question I asked myself," said Aimeric. "It is lost. It died with the last harpers of the Cumbrian kings. Their songs have endured, but not their learning. It is as lost as the Horn of Owain."

"Anything that is hidden can be uncovered," I said.

"Perhaps," said Aimeric, "but not in two days." He looked broodingly at his lute. "Nothing is worse than knowing there has once been wisdom and that it has been lost."

Orm had joined us and been listening. "I found what I was hoping to learn in Rath Sanas," he said. "The man who led the burning of Longthwaite is still alive and serving FitzDuncan. His name is Cathal Duff."

Aimeric and I exchanged glances. "We know him," I said. "He is the man we found lording it over Millom."

"What does he look like?" asked Orm.

"I'll tell you if we meet him again," I promised.

"It's only that I have a hunch," said Orm, "that when FitzDuncan finds we have vanished into the fells, Cathal Duff is the man he will send after us."

14. TAKING LEAVE

W e rode to Caerluel with all the pageant of a cavalcade with Robert de Brus and Griselle de Beauchamp at its head, but in the bustle of the city gate we made a quick parting, and I took the road to Allerdale with Orm Sigurdsson and Adele Espec.

With Adele beside me, the day before seemed like a bad dream. "Did your grandmother tell you all you hoped?" I asked.

"More," she replied, but that was all she would say.

"I liked your grandmother," said Orm. "Hard as flint, and she never wastes her breath."

Adele laughed. "Yes, that is my grandmother," she agreed. "Tell me about William FitzDuncan," she asked me. "What is he to you?"

I told her how I had first walked into his power, and he had thrown me straight into his dungeon – but there I grew confused, and found myself telling her more about Catriona.

"Love never dies," said Adele, "even when its flower has gone. I will always love Roger de Mowbray."

"And Robert?" I asked.

"Even Robert," said Adele.

"Then are we broken hearts," I asked, "torn too many ways to be held by one love?"

"I do wonder," she admitted, "but I asked you to tell me about FitzDuncan. Does our road pass Rath Sanas?"

"Not if I have my way," said Orm. "I'm told there's a bridge at a village a few miles downstream. That is where we'll cross the Derwent."

We left the road when we began to feel the shadow of Rath Sanas, and took to winding ways through woodland valleys. They brought us to Brigham, where we rode across the Derwent and into the village like butterflies into a web, for a band of armed men were watering their horses at the troughs on the green, and they sprang to bar our way.

"All who cross the Derwent pay a toll," one of them called out as we reined to a halt among their spears. I fumbled my wallet open and tossed three silver pennies at him. "Where are you bound?" he demanded.

"I have your master's safe-conduct," I told him. "He knows where I ride."

A figure stepped out of the doorway of the tavern; I glimpsed a gold disc-brooch encrusted with jewels and found myself face to face with Cathal Duff. He gave me a nod of recognition and feasted his eyes on Adele.

"If you're bound for Egremont," he said, "be warned that it's no place to linger." He gave us the semblance of a bow, and his men stood back. We heeled our horses and rode on.

"Now you know him," I told Orm once we were safely out of Brigham. "The man with the brooch was Cathal Duff."

"Good," said Orm. "I never forget a face."

"He had eyes like an adder," said Adele.

"Someone ought to drop a rock on his head," agreed Orm.

We hurried on, through the prospering villages of FitzDuncan's land and over the heath that made its border with the lost domain of Richard of Egremont.

Adele gazed in horror at the dragon-waste. She was so shocked that she did not speak until we came to the gaunt castle on its scorched hill.

"Is this what you endured in Northumberland?" she asked.

"It was never as bad as this," said Orm. "That was only war; this is hate."

We were greeted with a shout of joy by the watcher on the ramparts. The gates were flung open and we clattered over the bridge. It was the eeriest of feelings, entering so strong a castle knowing it all but defenceless and doomed to fall.

Richard and Maud were not in the hall to greet us. Ketel the steward made to lead us up to their eagle's nest high in the tower, but I told him I knew the way and took to the stairs with only Adele at my side.

Maud sprang to her feet as we entered the chamber of musty tapestries, but Richard rose stiffly, as if he had aged so much that it hurt him now even to move. While Adele and Maud embraced, the lord of Egremont clasped his hands behind his back and greeted me with a mask-like courtesy.

"We were beginning to believe you lost in the enchantments of Rath Sanas," he said.

Instead of trying to keep what I knew from showing in my face, I let him see it, and with a twitch at the corner of his mouth, a crack appeared in his emotionless mask.

"FitzDuncan has gathered his men," I said. "It is time we were leaving."

"Maud was ready yesterday," he replied. "See, her saddle-bags are packed."

"You are coming with us," I told him, "even if I have to tie your feet into your stirrups and your hands to your saddle."

"Which road will you take me by?" he asked wryly. "They are all watched."

"Yes," I said, "but while they are watching the roads, we will be crossing the fells."

"How?" he asked, and his mask slipped.

"Orm tells me there is a scarth at the head of Wastdale. We will be over before FitzDuncan even knows we are gone."

I gave him a moment for the vision to take hold in his mind's eye. The mask, and with it every trace of certainty, vanished from his face. He looked frightened of his own hope.

"Can you swear," he asked, "that if I run you will not despise me in your heart?"

"Yes," I answered without hesitation.

Richard smiled and shook his head. "I wish I could believe you," he said.

"You must," Adele said angrily. "Before the war, Simon was heir to a fine domain on the rim of the kingdom. He and his father held it against the Scots when all Northumberland had fallen, but when King David made its surrender a price of peace, they gave it up. Simon has left all he owned and become a landless knight to win peace for those he loved. If you had his courage, you would do the same."

I was as taken aback as Richard by her outburst, but I watched her words make their mark on him. The lord of Egremont made no reply. He looked at each of us in turn, and at Maud last and longest. She held out her hand, her fingers outstretched, and held it steady and pleading until he reached out and grasped it.

"Simon de Falaise," he said, "I entrust you with my deliverance."

Haltingly, with a voice on the edge of breaking, Richard told the gathered household of his choice.

"My treasure I leave with Ketel the steward," he said. "He will see that you each receive your share – but you are my greatest treasure, and I cannot take you with me. Those of you with no kin to return to will find sanctuary with the monks of Saint Bega. May God protect us all."

The true farewells were said face to face. I left them to it and went with Orm to the stables to prepare the horses for what promised to be the ride of their lives.

"That's the easy part done," said Orm. "Now we've cracked the nut out of its shell we have to protect it from the squirrels."

We paid no mind when one of the men-at-arms came and led a horse out into the bailey, but then we heard its hooves galloping over the bridge. Our eyes met over the saddle-bags.

"I wonder where that little squirrel is going to bob its tail," muttered Orm.

"This is turning into a nightmare," I said balefully.

"Not yet," said Orm. "FitzDuncan and Cathal Duff will put their heads together and guess we plan to slip across the Derwent at Brigham. I wish we had time to carve them a friendly greeting in runes."

We said nothing to the others, but as soon as they were ready we took the southern road. Orm and I rode either side of Richard, with Adele and Maud close behind. The wind was rising, but the clouds were high and bright and the roads dry. We travelled fast, and each mile took us further not only from Egremont but from Rath Sanas.

We came to the bridge over the river I now knew to be the Calder, and I could not cross it without thinking of the ruined abbey upstream. "Now there is peace," I said to Richard, "the monks will return."

"That is my one prayer," he said, "that Allerdale return to how it was when I first saw it."

"It will," I said, "in time."

Richard smiled bitterly. "All the folk of Allerdale care about their lord," he said, "is that he be lucky. If he is, he will give peace and law, and the land will prosper. If he is not, he will bring what I brought."

None of us wanted to say what we were thinking: that whatever else FitzDuncan might be, he was lucky; so lucky that in time the folk of Allerdale might even forgive him how he made himself their lord. Long after we were nameless dust, he would be remembered in the same breath as Ari Silkenbeard. His deeds would be sung and his cruelties forgotten.

In the distance we saw a man with a bundle of wood on his back. He was marching towards us, but he faltered when we came close enough for him to see our faces. He called out urgently to Richard and stepped into our path.

"Do I know you?" Richard asked him as we reined to a halt.

"Drew of Irton," he said. "Go no further, my lord. When I left Gosforth it was full of men-at-arms. They were set to ride north."

Richard thrust some coins into the man's hand, and he hurried on his way.

"We must go on," I said. "We have no choice. Gosforth stands at the gates of Wastdale. There is no other way."

"Then I will turn back," said Richard. "Without me you will be safe."

"No," I said.

"I would advise you to keep your head bare," Richard went on, "then they will not mistake you for me."

"No," I said, "we will find a way through."

Richard looked at me wearily. "I told you I was unlucky," he said.

"Not yet," said Orm. "There is one other way, though it will be harder going, and it means retracing our steps. Do you know Ennerdale?"

"I know it," said Maud. "I used to hunt there with my brother."

"There you are," Orm said to Richard. "With a wife like this, never call yourself unlucky." He winked at Maud and she burst out laughing. "Would you know a way there," he asked her, "that would spare us having to ride past Egremont?"

"There is a cattle-track that runs by Calder Abbey," she said. "I could follow it in the dark."

So we turned and made for the shelter of the fells. Maud led the way with Richard at her side, the lord and lady of the lost domain in flight through their own land. The track was wild and lonely, and we saw no one; but the hours were slipping by, and the man-at-arms who had left Egremont like a hare would be nearing the gates of Rath Sanas. I had a feeling that things were going from bad to worse, but when I glanced at Orm, I saw he was grinning.

"It's odd how you get to care for folk," he said. "Today is the first time I've heard Maud laugh. We've done the one thing I thought beyond us; we've made the lass happy."

15. THE RAINBOW BRIDGE

A t dusk we came to the gates of Ennerdale, a deep gash in the fells with a lake flooding its mouth. We were hurrying along the lake-shore when we came face to face with a lone rider, but he carried no weapons and heeled his horse aside to let us pass, doffing his cap when he saw there were ladies among us.

A sweep of cleared land stretched up the dale from the lake-head towards a steading I would have mistaken in the fading light for a heap of rocks had there not been a curl of blue smoke fraying above it. A wolfhound began barking from within its thick stone walls, but Maud rode straight up to the gate.

"Uncle Anlaf," she called. "Aunt Gudrun!"

A man stepped from the shadow of the wall, lowering the bow to which he had been fitting an arrow. A moment later we were inside, dismounting in the shaft of light from a door flung open. Maud was engulfed in the arms of a woman as round as a cheese, who greeted her with a torrent of reproach.

"If you had only sent word to warn us," she lamented, "I would have made you your cakes."

Maud turned to us joyfully. "Aunt Gudrun was my nurse," she said.

Anlaf was as thin and gnarled as his wife was not. They had a willowy daughter and a tubby son whose names were Ellisif and Wilf, and they would not even let us carry our saddle-bags; we were led to the hearth-bench, where Ellisif poured us ale while Gudrun pulled pastries and cheese and all manner of jars from her larder.

"I was the youngest," said Maud, explaining to Adele, "so when Mother judged I no longer had need of a nurse, she sent Aunt Gudrun home. I was so miserable without her that in the end Mother took pity on me. She decreed that every Easter week and Lammas, Uncle Anlaf would ride to Egremont and bring me back here."

"And I always had your cakes warm on the hearth-stone," said Gudrun.

"You used to run and hide when they sent to fetch you," said Anlaf.

"This was my secret place," said Maud. "Ranulf was the only one who shared it."

When she spoke her brother's name, Anlaf laid his hand on hers. "We'll not forget those days," he said.

"We have been out of our wits with worry for you," said Gudrun. "We hear such evil rumours."

"They will end now," said Maud. "We are leaving."

"Which road are you taking?" Anlaf asked worriedly.

"Over the fells," said Maud. "Orm is our guide."

"We're making for Borrowdale," said Orm. "We set out for the scarth at the head of Wastdale but found the road barred against us. I've been told there's a way from here over into the valley of the Gate Scarth. If there is, we'll take it."

"There are several ways," said Anlaf. "Come outside and I'll show you while there's still light."

I rose with them, and the three of us stepped out into

the yard. The moon was hidden by cloud and the fellsides were indecipherable walls of darkness.

"There's a path that leaves the head of the dale at the Giants' Graves," said Anlaf. "It will take you to the very neck of the scarth. There are quicker ways, but they take you over into the next dale with the scarth still to climb, and it is FitzDuncan's land. The men there answer to him. Wilf can go with you to make certain you do not stray; he knows the cairns and he can find his way home."

"Something is troubling you," remarked Orm. "Best spit it out."

"FitzDuncan will be after you," said Anlaf. "There'll be no hiding your tracks."

"We reckon," said Orm, "that he knows by now we're on the run, but he does not know which way we're running."

"He will by midnight," Anlaf said gloomily. "Did you meet anyone as you entered the dale?"

"A man on a horse," said Orm.

"That was Guddar," said Anlaf. "He's a great talker, and no fool. The chances are he is on his way to Rath Sanas on the hunch of a reward. If he is, FitzDuncan will be here by dawn."

"Then we'll not waste time trying to sleep," said Orm. "We'll be on our way as soon as we've eaten."

"You will never cross the fells in the dark," said Anlaf. "You need light to see the cairns. If you can be at the Giants' Graves by daybreak, it will be enough. You'll be in Borrowdale by sunset."

"Is Derwent Water in Borrowdale?" I asked.

"You know it?" asked Anlaf.

"I was there a year ago," I said. "There is a man named Thorald Armodsson who lives by the lake. He might give us shelter."

"Good," said Anlaf, "and if you cannot reach the lake before dark, there is a man named Erlend Siwulfsson at Rosthwaite. He hates Normans, but he has no great regard for FitzDuncan either."

The door opened behind us and Ellisif leaned out to call us in to supper.

We kept what we knew to ourselves, though the knowing made Anlaf's barley beer sit cold on my stomach. Maud was in high spirits, rekindling the past: Adele and the children listened entranced, but whenever she turned to share a memory with Richard, he surfaced from his own thoughts and forced a smile, a tired man who would rather have been staring into the fire.

I went out with Anlaf to make sure that the horses had settled, but also because I wanted to talk with him alone. In the lantern-lit stable I took my chance.

"How long have your kindred lived in Ennerdale?" I asked him.

"We go back," he said, "to the days of Ari Silken-beard."

"Two nights ago, I stood at his grave."

"Did you indeed?" said Anlaf. "What took you there?"

"We were searching for the Runes of Alnerdal. Do you know of them?"

Anlaf looked troubled. "All I know is that they are no longer in Rath Sanas."

"Why?"

"Because I knew the man who stole them."

"Is he dead?" I asked.

"Why are you searching for them?" asked Anlaf. "Do you want them for yourself?"

"I want them," I said, "so I can use them to bargain with the man who asked me to find them."

"FitzDuncan?" asked Anlaf, and when I nodded he let out a long muttering breath. "Forget it," he said. "You will never find them now."

"Who stole them?" I asked.

"Waltheof, the lord of Allerdale-below-Derwent. He was willing to let his nephew have Rath Sanas, but not its secrets."

"So he took the Runes from Ari's grave before he gave FitzDuncan the domain?"

"That is what he told me," said Anlaf. "He said that what he took from Ari's grave was a casket of walrus-ivory carved with runes."

"Did he read them?"

"He told me that he did not wish to," said Anlaf, "and there we quarrelled. I told him he had no right to take the Runes and hide them for no purpose. Ari left them for whoever had it written in his fate to find the Horn of Owain."

"Then you believe in it?" I asked eagerly.

"All I'm saying," replied Anlaf, "is that too many folk tried to thwart FitzDuncan when he was young, and they did it out of jealousy and fear, not out of wisdom. They made FitzDuncan the man he is, and their children have paid for it."

"What became of the casket?"

"I wish I knew," said Anlaf. "I'm told it was not among Waltheof's belongings when he died."

When I next stepped out of the house, it was still night, but Anlaf had roused us, and we were making ready to leave.

"Help me with this mail-shirt," said Orm, and as I laced him into it, he looked up at the cloud-filled sky. "You're in luck," he said. "You'll be hidden once you are on the fells."

"You talk as if you will not be with us," I said, knowing why but not wanting to.

"I'll be staying," he told me. "Anlaf and I are taking our bows down to the trees by the lake-shore to hunt squirrels."

"No," I said, "I need you with me."

"Cathal Duff will be leading the hunt," Orm reminded me.

"No," I pleaded, even though I knew his mind was made up. The others were ready and coming out of the house. When Orm saw my misery, he opened his arms, and for a moment we clung like bears.

"Get them safe over the rainbow bridge," he said. "I'll be hard on your heels if I've the luck, but if you meet a one-eyed wanderer with a raven on his shoulder, tell him to leave you alone and come looking for me."

He helped me mount and lifted Wilf up onto my saddle-bags. I could tell Maud was crying as she tore herself from Gudrun, but the darkness kept the others from seeing that Orm was not with us until we were out onto a track running up the dale.

"Orm's horse needs a shoe nailing," I lied before they had time to wonder. "He will follow."

We trotted upstream, the horses picking their way in the darkness. On every side we could hear the scouring of becks. When the sky began to pale towards daybreak we caught our first glimpse, through drifting cloud, of the ridges above us. The southern wall of Ennerdale was a dragon's spine, the northern a whale's back.

Wilf pointed excitedly over my shoulder. "There are the Giants' Graves."

They were grave-mounds, and they covered the floor of the dale like a fleet of upturned ships, huge, long, grass-covered and so ancient that every trace of their doorways had vanished.

I looked round anxiously. Beyond the graves, the ground rose in a bulge, a beck tumbling down to either side of it; and beyond and high above, the walls of Ennerdale met in a bow-shaped curve, blocking out the sky.

"If this is where our track leaves the dale," I said, "how does it do it? By wizardry?"

"Up there," said Wilf, and I almost sprained my neck trying to follow the line of his pointing finger. A swift-flowing beck had cut a gully down the fellside, and a path wound up it to vanish in the cloud.

"Now I know why Orm called it the rainbow bridge," I said. "It looks like a stairway to heaven."

It baffled the horses. We had to dismount and lead them by the reins, Wilf taking Adele's and Richard struggling with Maud's as well as his own. The women kilted up their skirts and led the way. I let my eyes follow Adele's nimble haunches and cracked my shin on a rock. After that I gave my mind to my footing and looked up only when I stopped to draw breath, which was often, for in the months since the Battle of the Standard I had slipped into the habit of letting horses do my walking for me.

We toiled up until the cloud rolled over us like a wave. Through its curling spray we had a last sight of the chasm of Ennerdale, then we passed into a world of grey shadows where shapes kept changing and I lost all sense of distance.

Wilf led the way. He waited for us at a cairn on a broad shoulder of fell where we met the wind. The cloud seethed around us; we could see another heap of stones like the one we stood shivering by, but no further.

Adele opened a saddle-bag her grandmother had given her and pulled out a flagon. It was bilberry wine, and we passed it from hand to hand, drinking like harvesters in the field. When Adele dug deeper, she found dried figs and a saffron and cherry cake, delicacies Agnes de Beauchamp must have been storing for the feast of Yule.

"We should save them," I warned. "We may need food tonight."

"There is more," said Adele, and at that we abandoned all restraint. We ate the cake down to the last crumb and walked on licking our fingers in the wind.

The path no longer led upwards, but across: we picked our way from cairn to cairn, tussock-stepping the bogs and stubbing our toes on the rocks. Our world had shrunk to the innards of the cloud. We could not see where we were heading, nor how far we had come. We went for so long at the same height that I grew convinced we had somehow turned a circle and were marching back towards Ennerdale – but then we reached a brow that curled over into a steep slope, and looking down I saw a cauldron-shaped high bare valley veined with becks and crossed by the dark rut of a track that looked wide enough to carry a cart.

"There is the Gate Scarth," said Wilf. "You have only to follow the track east to be in Borrowdale."

"We would never have found it without you," I told him.

Wilf looked at me keenly, blushing all over his plump cheeks. "Can I come with you?" he asked.

After a moment's disbelief, I saw myself through his eyes: a sword-begirt knight with a fine horse, a man worth following, all that when I was his age my father had seemed to me.

"I would take you gladly," I said, "but your kin need you more."

Richard reached into his wallet and gave Wilf so much

silver that his eyes went as round as the coins. "Few men must ever have needed a guide to lead them out of their own domain," he said. "Have I crossed my boundaries?"

"You are in FitzDuncan's domain now, my lord," said Wilf.

"Some would say I always have been," muttered Richard.

Maud kissed Wilf on the cheeks and he looked at her adoringly – as if that were the reward he would remember long after the silver coins were spent and forgotten – then he bowed to us in farewell and set off homewards.

As we gentled our horses onto the steep downward path, Adele caught my eye and smiled. "How could you turn him away?" she asked. "He would have followed you till the day you died, and grown into a man like Orm."

My heart gave a howl. I looked back, but Wilf had already vanished into the cloud.

16. THE LADY OF THE LAKE

O nce we reached the scarth track, we could ride, and we were soon in Borrowdale.

It was a wooded valley with steadings and villages in every crook of the land. We avoided them all and kept to an open track through fields of pasture and rye. The Derwent was here no more than a wide shallow beck winding in and out of reach, and we had to follow it through a ravine of moss and boulders before we came to the lake shimmering like a jewel in a crown of fells. It was just how I remembered it; there was even a plume of cooking-smoke rising from the hermit's isle.

For the last mile, I was the guide. We left the road for a path that crossed the marsh-meadows at the lake-head to the thick woods of the eastern shore, where we dismounted to lead the horses and found we were wooden-legged and weary. I was limping, and it seemed a fine irony to be hobbled in my flight by the wound I had been given in the Battle of the Standard by one of FitzDuncan's own men. I was beginning to feel I had been fighting him all my life.

"There is a boatman on the lake," said Maud.

He was rowing out from the hermit's isle, bound for

our shore. "That will be Thorald Armodsson," I said. "Last year he –"

"Look!" interrupted Maud. "Over on the fellside –"

Above the far shore of the lake we could see the ribbon of the track. The horsemen glinted with mail. They were riding from the north – from Rath Sanas. We were well hidden by distance and the shelter of the trees, and we watched as they rode down into the fields and along the very stretch of road we had just left.

When the last sound of their passing had died away, we hurried on and came to Thorald's landing-place just as he beached his keel. To my relief, he remembered me and greeted me warmly. He did not even bat an eyelid when he realised that four high and mighty Normans were throwing themselves at his mercy.

"We are being hunted by the men who have just ridden by on the far shore," I warned him. "If you do not want to risk giving shelter, show us a hiding-place in the woods."

"The only way you'll get a good night's sleep," said Thorald, "is if I row you out to the hermit's kell. I've a paddock set back among the trees where your horses will be safe."

He led us up to his house and we named ourselves to Hildi his wife. Adele opened her grandmother's saddle-bag and made our hosts a gift of a duck and venison pie, a wheaten loaf, and a jar of spiced fruit, all of which they at once insisted on sharing with us. We fed and settled the horses, and at dusk Thorald led us down to his boat.

"I will wait for Orm," I told the others.

"Then let me stay with you," said Adele, and I was too surprised and grateful to refuse.

We stood watching the others glide away to the sweep

of Thorald's oars. The clouds were breaking, and a hunter's moon had risen over the fells.

"I do not envy Maud," said Adele. "Richard is a wraith. His spirit is broken."

"He is wounded," I agreed, "but Maud will heal him."

"How?" asked Adele. "She hurts him without knowing it. Last night, when she spoke of her childhood, did you see his face? It tortured him to listen."

"Give the man grace," I said. "He has lost his domain. It hurt him to hear her speak of it with such love."

"No," said Adele. "What hurt him was that she was speaking of a different land. Did nothing strike you in what she said?"

"Only that they must have been golden years – when her brother was alive."

"Yes," said Adele. "Those are the years she longs for. That is her lost domain. She was able to leave without a backward glance because the Egremont she loved was lost years ago."

"It is true she is happy to be free," I admitted.

Adele smiled. "Listening to her," she said, "I saw into myself. You are the only person I know who may understand."

"Why?" I asked. "What did you see?"

"I have a lost domain," said Adele, her eyes dark in the moonlight. "I long for how it was when Mother was alive, before I ever knew I was a bastard or came to an age where it mattered."

I thought of my own mother and the village that had once been my world. "When you meet a man like Fitz-Duncan," I said, "it makes you grateful you grew up among kind and straight folk."

"I have been a fool," Adele said ruefully. "I have been looking for the knight who could take me back."

"And you have not found him?" I asked.

"How can I?" asked Adele. "We are all in exile. I know now that my mother's was worse. She lost her whole world the day she took to my father. She left everything."

"Why was her family so against it?"

"She was married to a man named Alan Waltheofsson," said Adele.

"I know of him," I said. "If you had been born his daughter, you would be the heiress of Allerdale-below-Derwent."

"With FitzDuncan for my kith and kin," said Adele. "I would rather be a bastard with no inheritance."

"There are worse things to be," I agreed. "So you do not regret that you came?"

"I do not know," she said, looking at me curiously. "Have I kept you from searching for Catriona?"

"Perhaps," I said, "but it changes nothing. Catriona is *my* lost domain. There is no way back to her."

"But are you still searching for one?" asked Adele.

"All I want to find," I said, "is a way to you."

Adele studied my face. "What do you want from me?" she asked.

"All you have to give," I said, and all my longing went into my words. It was sorcery to be so close to her, and for the first time I had the feeling that she knew it and was proud of it. She knew she did not even have to speak. She stood there, smiling into my eyes a look willing me to say more. "I know how it must have been for your father," I said. "I know why he was willing to break any law for the glory of holding your mother in his arms."

Adele breathed deeply. "This is how it must have been," she agreed.

I took her in my arms and she made no resistance, but she would not raise her lips to mine.

"What do *you* want from *me*?" I asked.

"I no longer know," she said. "I am frightened. I do not want to be cursed like my mother."

"How was your mother cursed?" I asked.

"She never gave birth to a son," said Adele. "To her that was God's judgement, that my father should have no son to follow him."

"You will never be cursed," I promised. "Tell me what you want in your heart."

"Simon," she said imploringly.

I tried to draw her closer, but all she would do was hide her face in my shoulder, and we stood there like a pair of herons. I stroked her hair. "What am I to do with all this longing?" I asked. "Throw myself into the lake until I cool?"

Adele laughed. "Do what you always do," she said. "Keep it hidden. How many secrets do you still keep from me?"

"None of the heart," I told her.

"Listen!" she said. "Did you hear it?"

I listened. A wavering call came from the trees by the lake-head. "It is only an owl," I said with relief.

"Is it?" asked Adele. She filled her lungs and made a hooting call that matched it like an echo. An answer came back along the lake-shore, and I understood.

"Wait here," I told her, "and answer the call if it comes again."

I set off along the path towards the head of the lake, and I had not gone far when I heard the ring of a horseshoe against a rock and Orm came walking towards me through the moonlit woods, leading his horse by the bridle. He grinned from ear to ear and gave me a hug that lifted me off my heels.

"Did you make a halt in Rosthwaite?" he asked.

"No," I said. "We rode on by."

"I got there at dusk," he said. "I was about to knock on Erlend Siwulfsson's door when I saw a line of tethered horses and figured it wise to tiptoe on my way."

"We saw the riders," I said. "We all but met them on the road. Did you meet with anyone else?"

"Hold out your hand," said Orm. I obeyed and he dropped into my palm a disc-brooch studded with jewels.

"Cathal Duff, wears a brooch like this," I said.

Orm took it back and stowed it in his wallet. "Cathal Duff," he said, "is feeding the ravens."

"What was the way of it?" I asked numbly.

"It was much like it is here," said Orm, "but in Ennerdale the track runs bare between the woods and the water. They came riding along it at daybreak and found the way blocked by fallen trees. They could not see us, but we had them outlined against the lake. Every arrow went to a good home."

"How many did you kill?" I asked.

"Seven," said Orm. "The rest rode out of Ennerdale faster than they rode in."

From behind us came the owl-cry of Adele. Orm chuckled and gave an answering hoot, and we turned towards the landing-place.

Thorald was there before us, back from the hermit's kell, and he greeted Orm as a fellow dalesman. As we walked up to the house, the two Cumbrians talked of folk they knew and for a moment I was alone again with Adele.

"What are you thinking?" she asked.

"Nothing," I said, and at once felt her disappointment.

"When will you trust me?" she asked plaintively. I reached for her hand but she slipped free and darted into the house. I felt like a troll trying to catch a unicorn.

I had been thinking of the killings, and wondering if somewhere there was a woman who would mourn for Cathal Duff.

17. THE RUNE-KEEPER

hile Adele fed Orm from the miraculous saddle-bag, I gathered my wits and turned to Thorald.

"Are we in Allerdale-below-Derwent?" I asked.

"We are," said Thorald.

"Then Alan Waltheofsson is your lord?"

Thorald shook his head. "Only in name. We are all under the shadow of Rath Sanas."

"Did you ever meet Waltheof, Alan's father?" I asked.

"I knew him well," said Thorald. "He often used to ride this way – and it is strange you should ask, for he has been in my mind since I met your good lady."

"Why?" asked Adele.

Thorald smiled. "In his later years, after his wife died, Waltheof used to ride here with a fine Norman lady. You remind me of her."

"She is my grandmother," said Adele.

"You're a carved likeness," said Thorald, slapping his knee. "She had an air about her. They say Waltheof wooed and worshipped her – he laid siege to her – but she never gave way."

"She still talks of him," said Adele. "They were great friends."

"I remember it all now," said Thorald. "Waltheof married his son to her daughter, but the daughter turned out to be a whore."

His wife turned white, and Adele gasped as if she had been struck. When Thorald understood what he had said, he groaned and hid his face in his hands.

"Forgive my husband," said Hildi. "He spoke out of loyalty."

"I would say the same," said Adele, "if my lord had been shamed."

"Still, I meant no insult," said Thorald sadly.

"I know why you were asking after Waltheof," Orm told me. "Anlaf said you were asking questions last night."

I nodded, but glumly. "I wish we had thought to ask Adele's grandmother," I said.

"We missed a chance there," Orm agreed.

"What are you talking of?" asked Adele.

"The Runes of Alnerdal," I replied. "Waltheof stole them from the grave of a man named Ari Silkenbeard. In your grandmother's chamber, did you ever see a casket of carved walrus-ivory?"

"I do not know," said Adele. "She has several caskets: one for needles, one for her treasures —"

"The one we are searching for will be old and ornately carved."

Adele shook her head. "What are the Runes of Alnerdal?" she asked.

I began the tale of our search with the night in Caerluel when FitzDuncan first asked me to find them, and she interrupted me almost at once.

"He came to Sablegarde," she said. "He told my grandmother it was time for him to have what belonged to him. She told him to get out."

"Then why did he not tell us if he thinks she is the one hiding the runes?" I asked.

"He wanted us to find our own trail," said Orm. "Mind you, by now he must think we have questioned her about them."

I thought back to my last words with FitzDuncan in the hall at Rath Sanas. He had been impatient to have me gone, and the barbed rumour about betrothals was the perfect weapon if his aim were to send me at once to Sablegarde, where he knew the runes might be hidden. If he had hurt me by design, to kick me on my way, it could only mean that there was a corner of his heart in which he wanted me to find the Runes of Alnerdal in time to save Richard of Egremont. I had made our bargain in the hope of finding a way out for Richard: now I wondered if FitzDuncan had made it in the hope of finding a way out for himself.

"I must go to Sablegarde," I said.

"It's a long walk," said Orm. "The horses are in no fit state, not if you want them to carry you to Greystoke tomorrow."

"I have horses," said Thorald. "They are smaller than your mounts, but nimble."

"Can we be there and back by daybreak?" I asked Orm.

"If we try," he said. "I can see you expect me to come with you."

"I'll need you to read the runes," I said.

"You'll need me to beg them from my grandmother," said Adele. "She may not wish to help you when she hears you want to give them to FitzDuncan."

"True," I said, "but she should at least be able to tell us why Waltheof wanted to hide them from him."

* * *

Stale riders on fresh horses, we were soon galloping past the sleeping villages of the lake-foot. The cold air stung our faces and made our eyes water, but there was an awesome beauty to the moonlit land. The fear I had felt leaving a warm hearth for the unknown night was blown away and its place taken by a sense of wonder. I felt as if an old magic were working itself out: as if we had only to abandon ourselves to it and it would carry us wherever it needed us to go.

Or so it seemed to me. Adele was locked in her own thoughts, and judging by her face they were troubled, while Orm was not about to abandon himself to anyone. He was using all his wits to find us a way across Cumbria that FitzDuncan's men might have left unguarded.

We were clear of the fells and well north of Rath Sanas when we came to the old straight road from Caerluel to Allerdale. To follow it would have been tempting fate, so we heeled our horses into the woods beyond and threaded the lanes from village to village until we came to the road I had ridden three days before.

It was well past midnight when we came in sight of Sablegarde on its knoll above the moonlit waters of the Solway. On the far shore I could see the forests of Annandale, and beyond and to westward the dark hills of Galloway.

There was a lantern glowing in the penticed walkway above the castle gate, and we were challenged as we rode up.

"Tell Agnes de Beauchamp," I called, "that Adele Espec seeks her help."

They unbarred the gate and let us into the bailey, where we waited until Agnes came out to us. She led us to the kitchens and ordered the servants who were sleeping there to serve us food and drink and then take themselves off to the hall. While they obeyed she filled three thimble-sized goblets with a dark potion that smelt of burning herbs and tasted of bilberries, and it drove the chill of the ride from our bodies in a single draught.

"What has happened?" she asked as soon as we were alone.

"Richard and Maud are safe on the hermit's kell on Derwent Water," I replied. "Tomorrow we will take them to Greystoke."

"I rejoice," Agnes said dryly, "though not sufficiently to be grateful for having been woken in the middle of the night to be told. Derwent Water is well within FitzDuncan's reach. They will not be safe until they are in Greystoke."

"The true reason we came," said Adele, "is that Simon is searching for the Runes of Alnerdal."

The old lady's face hardened. "Who told you of them?" she asked.

"William FitzDuncan," I replied.

"Has he sent you to shake them out of me?" she asked. "He has long believed I am their keeper."

"No," I said. "He challenged me to find the trail to them if I could."

"Do you know what they are?" she asked.

"Yes," I said. "They lead to the Horn of Owain."

"And you would give them to William FitzDuncan?" asked Agnes, giving me a look that could have curdled the milk of the Virgin Mary.

"I cannot answer that," I said, "until you have answered the question I came here to ask."

I paused and took a bite out of an apple to steady my nerves and give her temper a moment to cool.

"So," she said impatiently, "what is your question?"

"By what right did Waltheof rob Ari's grave and hide the runes?"

"It was not a matter of right and wrong," said Agnes.

"Then what was it?" I asked. "Because the more I know, the more it puzzles me. Ari Silkenbeard laid the runes for whoever wanted the Horn of Owain. Waltheof knew of them yet he never searched for the horn himself. Instead, he told his nephew – for FitzDuncan told me that it was Waltheof who told him the tale, when he was no more than a boy. FitzDuncan speaks of Waltheof as a beloved uncle, the man who gave him Rath Sanas. So why then, if Waltheof loved his nephew so well, did he start him on the search for the Horn of Owain only to tear the path from under his feet?"

Agnes smiled. "Yes," she said, "Waltheof loved his nephew all too well. FitzDuncan was everything his own son Alan was not."

Adele looked up with a start, and Agnes nodded sadly to her.

"Did he tell Alan of the runes?" I asked.

Agnes shook her head. "Only FitzDuncan. He was the one Waltheof believed born to follow them."

"What changed his mind?" I asked.

"He lived long enough," said Agnes, "to see Fitz-Duncan grow to manhood. Waltheof brought Alan and FitzDuncan up as brothers. His dream was that they would rule Allerdale together. FitzDuncan would be the fist and Alan the heart, and together they would save each other. Such was the dream."

"Was it FitzDuncan who broke it?" I asked.

"He was not the first," replied Agnes. Her gaze went up to the rafters, hung there a moment, then came down to brood on Adele. "When your mother ran away," she said, "FitzDuncan paid an Irish harper to sing to Alan's face that he was a cuckold. Waltheof never forgave him. He had already promised him Rath Sanas, but he took the Runes of

Alnerdal from Ari's grave. On the day he died he gave them to me and told me to keep them till FitzDuncan proved himself worthy of them."

"All these years you have been keeping the runes for FitzDuncan?" I asked in astonishment.

"For Waltheof's sake," she said. "I must admit I am beginning to despair. Shall I give them to you?" she asked Adele. "You would make a truer judge. Even if FitzDuncan were to put on a hair-shirt and vow penitence, I am too old and embittered to believe it."

Adele shook her head.

"FitzDuncan made a bargain with me," I said, "that if I find him the Runes of Alnerdal, he will let Richard leave in peace."

"Did he indeed?" asked Agnes. "Do you trust him to keep it?"

"Seven of his men were killed in Ennerdale yesterday morning," I said. "That was not in the bargain. He may say I broke it when I ran for the fells with Richard."

Agnes de Beauchamp rose to her feet. "It may well be," she said, "that all these years the Runes of Alnerdal have been awaiting their moment of purpose. Wait here and I will bring them to you."

She swept out and I grinned at Adele, but Adele was leaning forward on her elbows, her face hidden in her hands. I took hold of her wrists and tried gently to pull her hands away, but she resisted. Orm caught my eye and shook his head, and I let her be.

We were sitting in silence when Agnes de Beauchamp returned and laid on the table a small box as yellow as old teeth, its top and sides densely carved with figures and forms. There were stumpy-legged men and women with pin-pricked eyes, and a horse galloping unsaddled through a forest. Chiselled around the rim of the lid was a panel of runes.

"This is the casket Waltheof took from Ari's grave," said Agnes.

Orm took it and turned it in his hands, following the panel and nodding to himself.

"These are the Runes of Alnerdal," he said.

"What do they say?" I asked.

He read the runes again and laughed. "*To hold the Horn – shoot an arrow – through the ring – beneath Owain's chair.*"

"What does it mean?" asked Agnes.

"Aimeric may know," I said. "It means nothing to me."

"It hardly matters," said Orm. "The rest is for FitzDuncan to discover. This is your half of the bargain."

"Tell him," said Agnes, "that if he lets Richard leave in peace I will give him the satisfaction of taking the casket from my own hands."

"Thank you," I said. I stood up and every bone in my body creaked. "We must be on our way before we turn to stone."

Adele stared at us. "I must go to Alan Waltheofsson," she said. "I want to tell him how I wish it could have been otherwise."

"Leave him be," Agnes said sharply. "I have not even told him you exist, nor will I. Do you want to tear open his wounds?"

"No," Adele said miserably.

"You must take fresh horses," Agnes told us. "You may leave yours here in exchange."

"The ones we are riding belong to Thorald Armodsson," replied Orm.

"Tell him I will send a groom within a week to return

them," said Agnes; then she roused servants, had lanterns lit, and went with Orm to choose our new mounts. I kept with Adele. We waited in the bailey, gazing at the stars. They shone like crystals in the freezing sky.

"We know everything now," I said.

"Yes," said Adele, her face long and gaunt in the moonlight. "It is more than I can bear."

"It is what you came for," I reminded her.

"I came in search of my mother," said Adele, "and I have found her in myself. I know now why Father did not want me to come."

"He wanted you to keep your innocence," I said.

"No," said Adele. "He wanted me to keep my good name. He knew what folk would say if I ran off to follow you to Cumbria."

"What?" I asked.

She gave me the look she had given me on the lakeshore. "My aunts will be laughing behind their hands," she said, "telling everyone I am my mother's daughter."

"Does that trouble you?" I asked.

"Only for my father's sake," said Adele, and her face crept into a smile. "Why should it, now I know they are right?"

"It does not trouble me," I said.

"I know," Adele said ruefully. "I am beginning to think you were sent from hell to torment me."

Agnes and Orm returned with our new mounts and I fumbled with the buckles of girth-straps while Adele said her farewell to her grandmother. When all was ready and I turned to Agnes de Beauchamp to thank her again, she gripped my shoulder and kissed me on the cheeks.

"Cherish her," she said softly.

"Always," I promised.

"Now away with you," she commanded, and we galloped out of Sablegarde and south towards the fells.

18. THE RING OF STONES

I n the hollow moment between dawn and sunrise, the land turned the colour of ash. The tops of the fells were glowing like candles as we rode past the barking dogs of the villages at the lake-foot. By the time we reached Thorald's steading the sky was blue, but the long shingle-roofed house was still sunk in the frost-shadow of the night.

Thorald greeted us with great relief and set out at once in his boat for the hermit's kell. We slumped by the hearth, where Hildi ladled us bowls of salty kale-broth. I was so tired I had to soak my bread before I could swallow it.

A young man came in and greeted me gaily, and it was only when Maud came in behind him that I realised it was Richard. He squatted down beside me and grinned.

"Skuli the hermit sends you his greeting," he said. "That island is a holy place. I have never known such a feeling of sanctuary. I feel as if I have slept for a hundred years."

He wondered why we laughed. I told him how we had spent the night, though I took care to make no mention of my bargain with FitzDuncan.

Richard turned incredulously to Maud. "Have you ever heard of these runes?" he asked.

"No," she said, "but Alice once told me that Fitz-Duncan's mind is full of strange dreams. He measures himself against no man living, but against the heroes of the past."

"A legend in his own mind," muttered Orm. "They are always the ones who make the most trouble."

"But why does he want the Horn of Owain?" asked Richard. "What would he do with it?"

"He believes in its power," I said. "He believes it will give him the wisdom and wizardry it gave Ari Silkenbeard."

Thorald's head appeared abruptly in the doorway. "Riders," he said, "coming from the lake-foot."

A single leap took me over the hearth to the peg where I had hung my sword-belt. Three strides took me to the door. Orm joined me, his axe in his hand, and there we stood, blocking the threshold.

We could hear hoof-beats and the jingle of harness among the trees. Thorald was walking to the dung-heap to draw out his pitchfork when three riders came into the clearing. They were Aimeric, Arnoul and Hemming. Aimeric gave a yell of delight that set his horse prancing. I ran forward and grabbed hold of its bridle and the scholar almost fell out of the saddle into my arms.

"Thank God you're safe," he said.

"Why?" asked Orm. "Have you met with trouble?"

"None at all," said Aimeric. "All is well. Forne Ligulfsson is waiting to make you welcome."

"Then what are you doing here?" asked Orm. "We told you to wait for us at Greystoke."

"I came to find out if the hermit still lives on the island," said Aimeric. "He knows the past of Cumbria better than he knows the present. Think what he may be able to tell us about the Runes of Alnerdal."

Orm winked at me, and I said nothing. He shook his head. "There's no time for that, my lad," he told Aimeric. "We must be on our way."

Aimeric was appalled. "But we cannot leave without asking," he protested, and when Orm kept up a face of granite, the scholar turned to me with imploring eyes that broke my heart. "Believe me, Simon," he said, "we are so close. I have been learning the lost names of Cumbria. Forne told me of a man in Threlkeld, by whose hearth we slept last night. He taught me the names in the old tongue that mark the places where Owain's memory is kept. We are in the heart of his kingdom."

"Tell him," I begged Orm.

"We read the runes last night," Orm confessed.

"*To hold the Horn*," I recited, "*shoot an arrow through the ring beneath Owain's chair*."

Aimeric changed colour and stared at us. "There is a place I must take you," he said. "It lies on our road."

A cavalcade of eight, we climbed out of Borrowdale towards the long eastward-running glen at the far end of which lay Greystoke and the promised welcome of Forne Ligulfsson. I glanced over my shoulder as we crested the hill. There were folk on the roads, but they were all making for one of the villages by Derwent Water, where it looked to be market-day.

I turned to the road ahead, and saw the ring of stones.

The hill-top was broad and for the most part open heath. Sheep and goats were grazing, but there were no dwellings in sight. The stones stood upright in the heart of nowhere, magical by their pattern, dominating by their size. It was as if a giant had tried to take a bite out of the earth and his teeth had stuck fast in the ground.

"This is the place," said Aimeric. "Do you know it?"

"These are the Carles," said Orm. "Folk gather here on the nights of the winter-fire."

We rode into the circle, and the earth seemed to spin around us. We could see down into three different dales, but we were low enough to still be ringed by the high fells. The stones were like a herd of silent cattle.

"Aye," said Orm, "it's a place like no other. They say that however many times you count the stones of the circle, you'll never twice get the same number."

"Which way is north?" asked Aimeric.

"That way," said Orm, pointing to the wall of fells that stood between us and the plains of Caerluel.

Aimeric raised his own finger towards the fell that rose straight above us in hunched green and red shoulders. "Now, Orm Sigurdsson," he said, "can you name me that mountain?"

"That is Skiddaw," said Orm.

Aimeric smiled. "That must be the Viking way of saying a name grown old and meaningless. The true name of that mountain is Cadair Owain – the Throne of Owain. Now tell me if we are not at this very moment standing in the ring beneath Owain's chair?"

We had only to look from the weathered stones that encircled us to the summit of the great fell.

"The Horn must be here," I said.

"This is the ring," agreed Orm, "but none of us has an arrow, and none of us would know where to stand to shoot it."

My eyes were still on the high brown fell. "If I were looking down from the Throne of Owain," I said, "this circle would look as round as a straw target –"

Aimeric snatched the words out of my mouth: "– and

if you were to shoot an arrow through it, you would aim at the centre," he said. "The hub of the ring is the place to search."

While we sat in our saddles grinning at each other, Richard sprang down and strode towards a low stone that bulged out of the cropped turf like the boss on a shield. We hurried to dismount and follow, and only Arnoul and Hemming remembered their courtesy and waited to hold the stirrups of Maud and Adele.

"The perfect hiding-stone," said Orm, "just large enough for no one ever to move it without a reason."

He hacked out wedges of turf with his axe, and we saw that the stone was a slab and not a boulder. Even so, it took a while of cutting and five of us to lift the stone three paces west, revealing no more than bare soil and worms.

Orm got down on his knees and thrust his knife into the earth. It sliced in but jarred to a halt with a thumb's length of blade still between the ground and the hilt.

"A stone kist," he said. Richard and I dropped to our knees beside him and cut and shovelled until we uncovered the surface – then a corner – then all four corners of a green slate the size of an altar-bible.

"I'll tell you where we've seen stone like this before," said Orm. "Ari Silkenbeard's grave."

"There are runes," I said. I cleaned them out with my knife, then shuffled back to let Orm bend and read them.

"Six words," he said. "*Here waits the Horn of Owain.*"

Adele tugged at my cloak. "Leave it be, Simon," she urged me.

Her voice brought me to my senses, and I stood back. "Perhaps we should," I said. "It is enough that we have found it."

"I'll be damned if I leave it for FitzDuncan," said

Richard. "This is one thing he will never possess."

He lifted the slate and set it aside. It had been resting on four stones, and lodged between them was a crumpled leather pouch. Richard picked it up and pulled out the Horn – or the shape of it, for it was tightly bound in linen that had been rolled in wax, giving it a yellow skin that caught under Richard's fingernails as he flaked it off. We watched entranced as he peeled away the linen, revealing ancient silver chiselled with the patterns of wheel and spiral.

"That is no drinking-horn," protested Aimeric. "That is for blowing. Ari Silkenbeard said in the runes on his grave that it was for drinking –"

"Ari Silkenbeard," said Orm, "spoke in Viking poetry."

"There is only one way to drink from this," said Richard. He raised it to his lips and blew a peal that echoed from fell to fell until I thought Owain would appear on his throne high above us to ask why we had called him from his sleep: but it did not wake him, and Richard lowered the horn and smiled at Maud. "It is done," he said. "I have said my farewell to Cumbria."

Then we heard the answering call. It rang out behind us, from the floor of Borrowdale, and its cry was hardly lost in the wind before the sound of another reached our ears from away eastwards, down the road we hoped to ride.

"It seems there are folk out hunting," said Orm.

Richard looked around wildly. "Which way shall we ride?" he asked.

"You tell me," said Orm. "By the sound of it, they are at both ends of the road."

"We must stay here," said Aimeric. "We must stay within the circle. The harper told me that no man from Galloway will break the sanctuary of a ring of stones."

I had a feeling he was saying that for Maud and Adele. He knew as well as I did that men from Galloway burned churches and killed the folk inside when they ran out.

Orm was equally unimpressed. "Ride to those trees," he told Aimeric. "Take the women with you."

"No," said Aimeric. "We must stay within the circle."

We were silenced by the sight of the first hunting-pack cresting the hill. There looked about three dozen of them, and FitzDuncan rode at their head. They spread fanwise over the hill-top, scattering the sheep as they came.

"You may be about to meet Cathal Duff," Aimeric told Orm.

"We met in Ennerdale," said Orm. "Cathal Duff is feeding the ravens."

Aimeric's face fell even further. "So there has already been killing?" he asked.

"They have a few to avenge," agreed Orm.

Aimeric hitched up his cassock and ran towards the riders. I lunged to stop him, but Orm gripped me and held me back. By the time I had shaken myself free, it was too late: Aimeric had reached the rim of the circle and planted himself in the gap between two stones, his arms outstretched and his hands splayed, his dark tonsured hair and black cassock raked by the wind. He was shouting at the riders in what sounded like words of the old tongue, but he might as well have been singing to the fishes for all the difference it made to their gallop.

"No," cried Richard, and he started forward. I caught him by the arm and Orm grabbed him by the belt, and Maud joined us to hold him fast.

Aimeric stood his ground like a saint embracing martyrdom. I could not understand the words he was shouting, but I heard the ring of belief in his voice as it was drowned by the sound of thundering hooves.

The men of Galloway heard. They pulled back their horses' heads and bucked and jostled to a halt within a hair's breadth of the rim-stones of the circle, forcing Aimeric to at last step back. FitzDuncan shouted a command, but the riders ignored him. They drew away a short distance and came to a sullen halt, leaving FitzDuncan glaring in at us as though he were the one who was trapped.

"Come out like men," he shouted.

"Stay here," I told the others, and I limped to join Aimeric – who was as white as a maggot and shaking from tonsure to toe – and stand looking up into the furious face of William FitzDuncan.

"You seem to believe in pushing your luck until it breaks, Simon de Falaise," he told me.

"No, my lord," I said defiantly. "You are the one running that risk. You have the domain you craved. The price of it is that you let Richard go in peace."

"He will never have my peace," replied FitzDuncan, glaring over our heads at the grey-haired young knight who had withstood him for so long.

We all turned as more horsemen came over the eastern crest of the hill. Aimeric gave a croak of relief, and as they came cantering round the rim of the circle to where we stood, FitzDuncan greeted them as furiously as he had greeted us.

"You are a long way from your land, Forne Ligulfs-son," he said coldly.

"Let's just say I come to bear witness," replied the leader of the newcomers. He was a stout Viking of Orm's breed, armed, as were the seven men with him, and he gave his reply the cutting edge of a threat.

FitzDuncan looked at us in disgust, but he could not disguise that he was lost for words. Without the unthinking obedience of his hounds from Galloway, he was powerless. We were out of his reach.

He gave a shrug. "There is nothing here to witness," he told Forne. "I am chasing them off my land, that is all."

"I'll see them safely on their way," Forne assured him.

FitzDuncan looked at me with a grudging smile, and he was about to speak when from the centre of the ring of stones, Richard called his name.

"Come and talk," shouted Richard. "Come and say all that must be said."

FitzDuncan turned to me. "Do I have your safe-conduct?" he asked.

"You would trust a Norman's honour?" I asked.

"I want your word that he will not pull out a knife and spill my guts."

"He could be forgiven," I said, "but if he does, I will stand between you."

FitzDuncan dismounted and turned to Forne Ligulfs-son. "You can be my witness," he added drily.

We walked into the ring of stones, FitzDuncan at my side, Aimeric and Forne close behind. I saw that Richard had replaced the Horn of Owain in its leather pouch, which he held in his left hand. FitzDuncan could not know what it contained. He halted five paces from Richard and masked his face with a look of contempt.

"I have something you seek," Richard said gently.

FitzDuncan shook his head. "I have all I want from you."

Richard took a step sideways, revealing the open kist in the patch of earth laid bare. FitzDuncan stared at the slate chiselled with runes.

"How did you find it?" he asked.

"We read the Runes of Alnerdal," I said off-handedly.

"But how —" he started to ask, then checked himself,

as if it no longer mattered. He fastened his gaze on Richard. "What do you want in return?" he asked.

"I want our quarrel laid to rest," said Richard. "I will say now before witnesses that I am a landless knight and you are lord of Egremont, but let our children never know there has been hatred between us. For the love we owe our wives let us part in peace."

FitzDuncan stroked his moustache. "So I can pass Egremont to my son," he asked, "and you will not be breeding a pack of little Norman lordlings who will one day come to claim it?"

"More than that," said Richard. "Give him the Horn of Owain. Let it be the emblem of Allerdale, and I pray it brings you the wisdom of Ari Silkenbeard."

He was speaking now not for himself but for the lost domain he loved. FitzDuncan listened gravely, then turned to me. "And will there be peace between us, Simon de Falaise?" he asked.

I wondered if I could ever forgive him my wounds and all the misery he had made in the world, but the strangeness of it was that he needed to ask. William FitzDuncan was changing before my eyes from a man with a hundred grudges and everything to win into a man with everything to lose. He no longer wanted enemies. I thought of all Alice had told me of the childhood scars that had haunted his life, and for a moment even wondered if he were the one of us who would need the most healing.

"There will be peace unless you break it," I told him.

FitzDuncan glanced at Forne Ligulfsson. "I hope you are witnessing all this," he said, but the irony went from his voice as he turned back to Richard. "I am minded to accept your bargain."

Richard held out the leather pouch. FitzDuncan took

it and drew the Horn of Owain out into the daylight, his eyes widening when he saw the beauty of its workmanship. He raised it to his lips and shivered at its touch, then laughed at himself and blew a long rallying call which echoed against the fells but went unanswered.

"The hunt is over," he said. His gaze swept round our faces; he bowed to Maud and Adele; then he strode to his horse, swung up into the saddle with the Horn still clasped in his hand, and rode for Borrowdale. The men of Galloway raised their reins and heeled their horses after their lord. I wondered how long they would follow him.

We rushed to Aimeric, who looked as if he were about to faint.

"That was brave," Adele told him.

"It was sorcery," said Aimeric. "I was possessed."

"We have all been possessed," said Maud.

She and Adele led the shaken scholar to his horse. I turned with Richard to help set the hiding-stone back in its place and tread the turf down along its edge. We worked hurriedly, and said little, for we suddenly felt as if the stones were watching us; waiting for us to be gone; waiting to recover their silence.

19. THE BANQUET OF DELIVERANCE

W hen darkness fell we were in Forne Ligulfsson's manor of Greystoke, where the fire burned bright and the ale was strong.

Aimeric had sent word to Orm's kinsfolk at Longthwaite, and they rode over to join us. Three years had gone by since Orm had last seen them, and a year since Aimeric and I escaped from Caerluel with Hoskuld and Arni, so we greeted each other joyfully – and I found myself face to face with Sigrid. We kissed each other's cheeks and I gazed at her.

"How is it," I asked, "that you are more beautiful each time I see you?"

"You must be going blind," said Sigrid. "You should have seen me at Michaelmas. I was as fat as a bullock."

Then I remembered, and looked her up and down. She wore her gown loosely belted, and her breasts were full. "Catriona told me you were with child," I said.

"He is safely born," said Sigrid proudly.

"A son?" asked Orm. "This calls for a celebration. What have you named him?"

"Simon," replied Sigrid.

Arni her husband came and put his arm around her,

grinning at me. "What other name could we give him," he asked, "when we know that if you had not saved me from FitzDuncan's dungeon, he would never have been born?"

"We want you to be his godfather," Sigrid told me. "I know you will be all my brother Thord would have been to him."

"I will be honoured," I said gratefully.

Orm reached into his wallet and held the jewelled disc-brooch out to his brother.

"I have seen this before," said Hoskuld. He looked up with a deepening frown. "The man who killed Thord and ordered the burning of our halls wears a brooch like this."

"His name was Cathal Duff," said Orm. "I gave him to the ravens."

"Then it is finished," said Hoskuld. "Let us drink to the new-born."

Sigrid searched my face with her Viking blue eyes. "I was hoping," she said, "that Catriona would be with you."

"Have you seen her?" I asked.

"She left here last spring," said Sigrid. "She went to search for you."

"She found me in high summer," I said. "We walked the length of Northumberland, then she left me at the gates of Tynemouth Priory."

"How did you part?" Sigrid asked curiously.

"She said our paths may cross again," I replied, "but it was not a promise."

"She told me once," said Sigrid, "that she believes she is fated to destroy you."

"Catriona said that?"

"She has the second sight," said Sigrid. "She told me that my child would be a boy."

At that moment we were joined by Adele and Aimeric.

I reached for Adele's hand, and she clasped mine tightly and smiled.

"Forne says he will lend us fresh horses for the ride to Caerluel," she told me happily.

"We are not going to Caerluel," I replied. "We are taking the shortest road home, and that lies eastwards."

"But I promised I would be there," Adele protested.

"When?" I asked.

"Tomorrow," she said, looking at me as if that made everything clear. "Tomorrow," she repeated, "for Robert's wedding."

The bells of Saint Mary's were ringing out over Inglewood as we came in sight of Caerluel. They fell silent before we were through the city gates, and by the time we reached the priory yard it was empty of all but a few grooms minding the horses.

Straightening our buckles and folds, we hurried through the great arched doorway into the church. In the crowded nave, Adele reached for my hand to draw me aside and hold me back while the others made their way forward to join the gathering of nobles by the altar.

"We will see nothing from here," I warned her.

"We must talk," she said, pulling me into the shadow of a pillar close to some pious women who clucked their tongues disapprovingly.

"What is it?" I asked.

"The world is about to swallow us," said Adele. "When will we next be alone? What task will Thurstan have waiting for you when we return?"

"As soon as we get back to Elmeslac," I said, "I am going to ask Walter to give you to me in betrothal."

"No," said Adele, with a long shake of the head. "We can never be married."

"Why not?" I asked.

"Because it would not be right."

"How can you say that?" I asked. "Have you forgotten the lake-shore? That is the threshold where we stand. All I want to know is how to cross it."

The look on my face made her smile, but then she groaned and laid her head against the pillar. "It is true," she said, "that I am yours if you are mine, but you would be making a great mistake if you gave yourself to me."

"How?" I asked.

Adele frowned at me. "Robert says you are held in honour by men like King David. He says you will win great fame. If you wait a few years you could win yourself an heiress and father a dynasty. I would give myself to you for those few years and never regret it, but I cannot bring my father the shame of seeing his daughter become a knight's concubine."

"I am not asking you to be my concubine," I protested. "I want to marry you. I want the blessing of the Church on our children."

"Even if I bring you no dowry?" asked Adele.

"All I want," I said, "is a domain of the heart where I live to the full with those I love, and you are the woman I want to be my wife."

In the choir beyond the altar, a penitent chant came to an end and the canons raised their voices in a hymn of joy. It would soon be the moment when Robert and Griselle received their blessing.

"If it could only be done before we return," said Adele, and a moment later, without another word spoken, we were walking hand in hand from pillar to pillar along the side-aisle, until we were within a few paces of where Robert and Griselle were kneeling.

The hymn came to an end and Bishop Aethelwold turned towards them. Adele squeezed my hand, and with our eyes fixed on Robert and Griselle we stepped from the shadows, walked past the gathered nobles and knelt together on the altar steps. There was a moment of startled hush, broken by Robert and Griselle's cries of delight; then behind us in the nave there were some ribald exclamations, and one was from a voice oddly familiar.

Bishop Aethelwold loomed above us, waiting for solemnity to return.

"We ask the blessing of holy Church," I said. "We ask to be married."

"It is customary," the bishop told us, "for the blessing to follow the betrothal." He looked out over our heads. "Will anyone here bear witness that the father of this woman consents to her marriage?"

"I consent with all my heart," answered the voice of Walter Espec.

We turned and saw him in a crowd of faces we knew, my father among them. Mostly they were Robert's kinsfolk from Yorkshire, and I guessed they must have ridden over Stainmoor to be at the wedding. Too late I realised what we had done. With Griselle's kin were half the nobles of Scotland, and her mother was glaring at us as if to say that two bastards had no right to intrude on the ceremony that would bind together the dynasties of de Brus and de Morville: but beside her was Agnes de Beauchamp, and the old ogress gave her grand-daughter a nod of approval and a look that no longer disguised love.

Adele turned back to me, so sure of herself now that I felt scorched by her sense of purpose.

"No more secrets," she begged me. "Let me always know where you are and what has taken you there."

"You will," I promised.

Bishop Aethelwold joined our hands and made the sign of the cross over them. When he blessed us, he spoke in Latin, so I could not understand his words. They did not sound a spell of any great power against the witchcraft of love.

The wedding-feast was magnificent. At every table, from one end to the other of the great hall of the castle of Caerluel, men from Scotland and Northumbria sat together, men who a few weeks before had been enemies at war. Even Walter Espec and Agnes de Beauchamp sat together, finding at last, in Adele, a joy they could share.

All of this was Hugh de Morville's doing. He had never been a man to miss a chance of enhancing his own reputation, and he was making the most of his daughter's wedding. Many of the lords of Cumbria were there – but not William FitzDuncan. I would have liked him to see my hour of glory, but I was proud enough when Hugh de Morville gave places of honour to Richard and Maud.

For me there was a single shadow, and it was cast by a man I had never seen before. He sat towards one end of the high-table, showing no interest in the fine food on his trencher, nor did he seem to be answering what folk said to him. Instead, he sat gazing at Adele, his eyes full of torment. She was too caught up in our knot of friends to notice, but it troubled me.

Just before dusk, the ladies rose and drew the brides away to make them ready for their leave-taking. Robert and Griselle were riding to Annandale. Orm and Forne Ligulfsson had already set out for Greystoke to prepare a bridal chamber and a Cumbrian welcome for when Adele and I rode in, escorted in cavalcade by Jordan and Aimeric, Arnoul and Hemming.

The stranger watched Adele go, sitting forward for a last glimpse of her as she passed through the doorway that led to the women's chambers. The feast at Caerluel was far from over – the toasts and singing were just beginning, and Aimeric was tuning his lute with an impish look on his face – but the stranger stood up and pulled his cloak around his shoulders. In a flat voice he thanked Hugh de Morville for his hospitality, and as he turned to leave he gave Walter Espec a silent nod of greeting.

"Who was that, my lord?" I asked my father-in-law.

"His name is Alan Waltheofsson," Walter replied guardedly. "Do you know him?"

I felt as if I knew him. Alan Waltheofsson was the man from whom Walter had stolen Adele's mother. I knew then that he had not been gazing at Adele to wish her evil. He had been staring into his lost domain.

Two days later, I rode with Adele at my side up the steep western slopes of the Stainmoor.

At the Kings' Cross we drew rein to look back. The Vale of Eden stretched below us in sunlight, but the distant fells were hidden by cloud. The wind was bitter, and most of our cavalcade jingled on by, but others joined us two by two, until the eight of us who had stood together in the ring of stones were reunited. There was little to say, but it was not through emptiness. We all felt the brotherhood that bound us now, the brotherhood forged in a few short winter days in Cumbria.

"This is the moment," said Aimeric, "when we must put FitzDuncan behind us for ever. If any of you still hate him, curse him now with all the words you can find, but then we must ride away."

Even Richard shook his head. I wondered. William

FitzDuncan was the greatest force of evil I had ever met, but where once he had seemed unknowable and unbreachable, now I could almost see into his mind. There was too much I understood for me to curse him. The last thing I wished him was another curse.

"There's snow in those clouds," said Orm, his eyes still on the distant fells, "and they'll be with us by nightfall."

We turned homewards, the wind at our backs.

KNIGHTS OF
THE SACRED BLADE

Julian Atterton

In the warring Britain of 1135, the kingdom of Northumbria faces destruction. Young Simon de Falaise and Aimeric the scholar set out on a perilous quest to find "The Sacred Blade" – an ancient sword with the power, according to legend, to save their homeland. Others, however, are also searching...

"Julian Atterton is one of the brightest stars in the galaxy of young historical writers."
Christina Hardyment, The Independent

"Julian Atterton writes with power and clarity, his clean-cut prose glinting with flashes of poetry."
Geoffrey Trease
The Times Educational Supplement

"Political intrigue, romance and deeds of courage are woven together in this fast moving tale."
Valerie Bierman, The Scotsman

BROTHER NIGHT

Victor Kelleher

He looked up and saw two pale half-moons. Two! Eyes staring at him. A face hanging there in the gloom. So awful a face that he screamed and screamed again...

Ramon has been brought up as the son of a village gate-keeper. One night, though, he is told his true parentage: his mother is the Moon Witch and his father the all-powerful Sun Lord. More disturbing still, he learns that he was one of twins, his monstrous brother apparently destroyed at birth. But nothing, as Ramon soon discovers, is this black and white – what seems dark may be light, what seems good may be evil. One thing, however, *is* certain: finding out the truth is going to be a very perilous and challenging quest indeed...

"A robust and thought-provoking fantasy... Powerfully imagined... Fast paced and full of action."
Neil Philip
The Times Educational Supplement

CALABRIAN QUEST

Geoffrey Trease

Her heart nearly stopped… The figure was human – but the head upturned to meet her incredulous stare was the head of a wolf.

A fifth-century Roman christening spoon is the catalyst for this thrilling adventure which sees Max, a young American, travel to Italy with Andy, Karen and her cousin Julie on a quest for lost treasure. It's not long, though, before they encounter some sinister happenings and find themselves in conflict with the local Mafia…

"A gripping story of archaeological adventure… The tale rattles along, demonstrating an unputdownability as durable as [Geoffrey Trease] himself."
Mary Hoffman, The Sunday Telegraph

"From storytelling such as this, readers are infected with a love of books."
Jill Paton Walsh
The Times Educational Supplement

A BOX OF TRICKS

Hugh Scott

"Simon Welkin! Come! We would converse with thee!"

Every summer, John and Maggie are packed off to stay with their Aunt Nell and Great-grandfather Harris in the country. But this year they get an explosive surprise, when Great-grandfather decides to waken the dead!

"Hugh Scott is at his best, stretching and exciting the imagination, producing glittering effects... Eerie and occasionally terrifying, beautifully evoking dark and light... The tension mounts to make the pulse race."
Susan Hill, The Sunday Times

"Horror-hungry 10-year-olds will love it."
The Sunday Telegraph

"A book which will be read again and again – a captivating ghost story which could well become a classic."
Time Out

SHADOW OF THE WALL

Christa Laird

"There's only one way which is reasonably safe, Misha, and it's not very pleasant." Misha sat back on the pile of newspapers... Sheer physical panic seized him, beginning in his feet and rising up like an electric current through his limbs.

"Not ... not the sewers?" he croaked.

It's spring 1942, and life in the Warsaw ghetto is hard and often brutal, with the Jews subject to beatings and execution at the hands of the hated SS. Young Misha lives at the Orphans' Home run by the heroic Dr Korczak. But the time is f approaching when Misha must r himself a hero too...

"A story full of exciter passion."
Geoffrey Trease
The Times Edu

"A book
Jessica Yat

"N
this
huma
Naom

"Janet Lu
The Times

SHADOW IN
HAWTHORN BAY

Janet Lunn

*Softly she began to sing in Gaelic a song
for the dying, and as she sang she stepped
off the rock into the bay. She walked out
until she stood waist-deep in the water.*
"I am coming, mo gradach, *I am coming
to where you are."*

Fifteen-year-old Highland girl Mary
Urquhart has the gift of second sight. One
spring morning in 1815 she hears the voice
of her beloved cousin Duncan calling to
her from three thousand miles away in
upper Canada and knows that somehow
she must go to him. It is to prove a long
and perilous journey, however, and Mary
encounters much heartbreak and adversity
before her quest finally comes to an end.

"Memorable … haunting… In one sense
…is a ghost-novel – but it is also true to
…n behaviour."
    …i Lewis, *The Observer*

"…nn tells a compelling tale."
    …Educational Supplement

THE LAST CHILDREN

Gudrun Pausewang

It's the beginning of the summer holidays and the Bennewitzs are on their way to visit grandparents in the mountains. Suddenly, there's a blinding light in the sky – and the Bennewitzs are on the road to hell...

Shocking, distressing, brutally honest, this fictional account of the aftermath of a nuclear holocaust has already profoundly affected thousands of readers in Germany. Read it and it will change you too.

"This disturbing book shouldn't be limited to the teenage market but should be compulsory reading for most adults, especially those in positions of power."
Judy Allen, The Sunday Times

MORE WALKER PAPERBACKS
For You to Enjoy

☐ 0-7445-2042-8   *Knights of the Sacred Blade*
by Julian Atterton   £3.50

☐ 0-7445-2331-1   *Brother Night*
by Victor Kelleher   £3.99

☐ 0-7445-2304-4   *The Calabrian Quest*
by Geoffrey Trease   £2.99

☐ 0-7445-3085-7   *A Box of Tricks*
by Hugh Scott   £2.99

☐ 0-7445-1759-1   *Shadow of the Wall*
by Christa Laird   £2.99

☐ 0-7445-2000-2   *Shadow in Hawthorn Bay*
by Janet Lu

☐ 0-7445-1750-8   *The Last Cl*
by Gudrun

☐ 0-7445-1781-8   *Knight Afte*
by Sheila S

Walker Paperbacks are available from most bo
by post: just tick the titles you want, fill in
Walker Books Ltd, PO Box 11, Falmou

Please send a cheque or postal order and allow the
UK & BFPO – £1.00 for first book, plus
plus 30p for each additional book to a r
Overseas and Eire Customers – £2.00 for first b
plus 50p per copy for each ad
Prices are correct at time of going to press, but ar

Name _____

Address _____

_____